Merry Christmas 1990
Summer

Love from Mom

OPHELIA'S ENGLISH ADVENTURE

or

THE HAUNTING *of* BRUINYES HOUSE

OPHELIA'S
ENGLISH ADVENTURE
or
THE HAUNTING of BRUINYES HOUSE

by MICHELE DURKSON CLISE

Text with JONATHAN ETRA

Clarkson N. Potter, Inc./Publishers
DISTRIBUTED BY CROWN PUBLISHERS, INC., NEW YORK

Also by Michele Durkson Clise

*Ophelia's Voyage to Japan: Or, The Mystery
of the Doll Solved*
*Ophelia's World: Or, The Memoirs of a
Parisian Shop Girl*
My Circle of Bears

Published by Clarkson N. Potter, Inc., 225 Park
Avenue South, New York, New York 10003, and rep-
resented in Canada by the Canadian MANDA Group

CLARKSON N. POTTER, POTTER, and colophon
are trademarks of Clarkson N. Potter, Inc.

Manufactured in Japan

Library of Congress Cataloging-in-Publication Data

Clise, Michele Durkson.
    Ophelia's English adventure, or, The haunting of
Bruinyes house.
    Summary: Ophelia B. Clise, the proprietress of the
Bazaar des Bears, finds new adventure with her
friends when they accept an invitation to tea with the
Queen of England.
    [1. Teddy bears—Fiction. 2. Mystery and detec-
tive stories] I. Etra, Jonathan. II. Title. III. Title:
Ophelia's English adventure. IV. Title: Haunting of
Bruinyes house.
PS3553.L567O57   1987   813'.54 [Fic]   86-25454
ISBN 0-517-56558-7
10 9 8 7 6 5 4 3 2 1

First Edition

To Marsha Burns,
for her generosity of
spirit

Zenobia, Ophelia, Conrad, Ricky, and Yukiko

I

It was ten o'clock and the postman was late, which always annoyed Ophelia, most especially on Monday. After a whole weekend without mail, it was irksome to wait until eleven or twelve o'clock in the morning to hear from the rest of the world. Ophelia and her friends had just returned from exotic Japan.

They had gone there to rescue Yukiko, the beautiful Japanese doll Schnuffy had bought for Ophelia, from the clutches of the unscrupulous doll maker Mr. Ningyosan. At the same time, Dr. Churchill had recovered a spectacular pearl lost a hundred years before from the British royal crown. Of course he had returned it to the Queen of England, and in gratitude for the bears' help, the Queen had promised to invite them all to tea. Certainly the invitation would arrive today. But where was the postman?

Ophelia folded and refolded the bath towels and handkerchiefs, the bedspreads and pillowcases, not to mention picking up and putting down the back scratchers, bed warmers, tea cozies, turbans, toy trumpets, fans, feathers, lace ribbons, very large spoons (for making bouillabaisse), very tiny forks (for eating canapés), and those little

rolling brushes for getting the crumbs off the table after a particularly crumb-filled meal. Ophelia B. Clise was the proprietor of Bazaar des Bears, the shop on Paris's rue du Bac that specialized in everything and anything a bear might desperately, passionately, or certainly occasionally need. All the best bears shopped there and more than a few of the worst. Ophelia knew that some of the worst bears made the best friends.

"Please stop fidgeting," begged Zenobia Onassis, Ophelia's close friend and partner and Bazaar des Bears' ever-efficient bookkeeper. "You know it makes you hungry and it's still hours 'til lunch."

"I don't understand why the postman is always late when something wonderful is coming in the mail. If I knew it was just going to be bills and advertisements for antiques shows I wouldn't care. But our invitation is coming from *the Queen of England!*"

"We could send Ricky around the corner for *mille feuille* or perhaps a *pain au chocolat* or . . ." Zenobia suggested cautiously. She knew how undependable Ricky Jaune, the young shop concierge, could be once sent out on any errand more than fifty feet from the door of the store—the lure of the pinball machines at the corner tabac could sometimes result in Ricky's disappearance for the entire day.

This suggestion only renewed Ophelia's state of distress. "The best possible assortment of letters and postcards from all over the world, from Schnuffy and Mona Lisa in Japan, Dr. Churchill and Aunt Vita in England, Popie and Marcello in Rome, and any number of other remarkable people in one thousand and seven wonderful places, is about to arrive," exclaimed Ophelia in one tremendous breath. "And here we sit doing nothing, waiting helplessly." She plopped down in a chair, almost demolishing a box of bow ties and an Emmenthaler sandwich belonging to M. Ritz, the shop watchmouse.

"If you want the sandwich," he squeaked, "you can have it. But I think you would enjoy it more unpressed."

"I'm all right," sighed Ophelia, clasping her paws tightly, biting her lip, overturning a rare china cup with an elbow, and kicking a small damask pillow halfway across the floor. Fortunately, at this very moment the doorbell rang. In sauntered Conrad, back from Vienna where he had designed the costumes for the State Opera's gala production of *Aida*. He wore a new green silk coat and in his hand was a large package of colorful postcards and beautifully engraved envelopes.

"I met Monsieur Gris, the district postman, on my way. He insisted I bring these to you at once. There's a very important letter here." Conrad plucked a splendid vellum envelope from the midst of the pack and handed it to Ophelia. A large foil seal in gold surrounded by red and blue ribbon was immediately visible. Ophelia began dancing through the store holding aloft her prize.

"I knew it. I knew it. Here it is," she shouted.

"Open it quickly," cried Conrad, dancing with her and trying to get a better look at the envelope. Ophelia, barely standing still, undid the flap and extracted the hand-engraved card. She read the words out loud: "Her Royal Highness, the Queen of England, requests the pleasure of your company for tea on Tuesday, 3:30 P.M., the 24th of June. Regrets only. Buckingham Palace, London, England." Down in the lower right corner was a little postscript in what Ophelia recognized as the Queen's own fragile hand, "Please bring six lace doilies in blue and five of your best red pillowcases—don't tell the Prince—Love, H.R.H." Ophelia smiled. "What a lovely woman. Everybody pack. We're going to England!"

"It's lucky I got this new coat," said Conrad, twirling around in it for the ladies. "It looks fabulous against a white marble background."

Her Royal Highness, the Queen of England
Requests the pleasure of your company for tea
Tuesday 3:30 P.M., the 24th of June
Regrets only
Buckingham Palace, London, England

"How clever," agreed Zenobia admiringly. "Where did you get it? It must have cost a fortune."

"Not at all. I borrowed it from next year's production of *The Magic Flute*. I promised to have it back in Vienna for the fall season. But I may not," he added sheepishly—which is very hard for a bear.

Conrad's new coat

"It's magnificent," said Ophelia, touching the soft, plush fabric. "It goes so well with your red scarf."

"He looks like a traffic light," said Ricky Jaune, poking his head in from the store-room and waving a monumental feather duster in the air for emphasis before retreating.

Clarence appeared from his study. "What's all the excitement?" he asked. "Did we win the lottery?" Clarence, Ophelia's *cher ami*, was a renowned food critic. He was often buried deep in his library researching the origin of mustard or the future of toast, when not out and about reviewing the restaurants of Paris.

"The Queen has invited us all to tea," explained Ophelia.

"How lovely," cheered Clarence. "I'm hungrier than a truffle hound on his tenth truffle." Truffle hounds never get to eat the truffles they find. After a long day of finding truffles and not eating them, you'd be very hungry indeed.

"It's not 'til tomorrow," put in M. Ritz. "You can have part of my sandwich, but it's somewhat flat."

"It's time to go shopping," said Ophelia, springing toward the cash register to see how much money was there. "I have nothing to wear."

"We don't have any room in the budget for unnecessary expenditures," wailed Zenobia. "The rent is due. We need to fix the stairs to the cellar. We spent twice as much as we should have on the new rug and the silk kimonos Mona found in Japan."

"It's the Queen of England. We must look our best. I saw the most beautiful pink ball

gown at the Marché aux Puces," sang Ophelia, her eyes afire.

"You don't wear a ball gown to tea," corrected Conrad.

"What if there's dancing?" said Ophelia.

"Nobody dances before nine P.M.," Zenobia insisted.

"I've gone dancing at one in the afternoon," explained Clarence. "It's called a tea dance."

"We're not invited to a tea dance. We're invited to tea," Zenobia groaned.

"It's best to be prepared." Ophelia smiled. Poor Zenobia, she always tried. The success of the store was due so much to her careful, scrupulous attention to every last centime. Ophelia, who adored the good things in life—caviar, chocolate, Le Nôtre's, Poilânes, and silk ribbons—was all too prone to let the francs fly.

"It's probably freezing in London this time of year. Perhaps I'll also need a new coat . . ." Ophelia speculated, eliciting further distress from Zenobia.

"I doubt that will be necessary," Clarence assured her. "Summer in England is quite beautiful. There are roses everywhere, and lilies, and bushes called topiary in the shapes of animals."

"The bushes grow in the shape of animals? How clever," said Zenobia, thoroughly pleased. "I should like to see that."

"They're *trimmed* to look like animals. You can't rightly expect a bush to grow into an elephant all by itself," said Conrad.

"I don't see why not. We grow into bears by ourselves," said Zenobia.

"We *are* bears," said Ricky Jaune, reappearing. "If we were bushes, we would grow into bushes."

"Speak for yourself," said Zenobia. "As far as I'm concerned, I'd always be a bear. Even if I were a bush."

"We'll have to bring gifts for the Queen," thought Ophelia out loud, "and we'll need someplace to stay in England."

"And we should see some of the sights—the British Museum, the Tower of London, the theater," added Clarence.

"It would be fun to see some of the shops," said Zenobia.

"And the rock stars," said Ricky Jaune. "The Rolling Stones came from England."

"They're in America now," corrected Conrad. "At least some of them."

"But they came from England. The Statue of Liberty may be in New York, but it came from France."

"Everything came from France," observed Ophelia. "Foie gras, champagne, croissants, Chanel, *l'amour*."

"Chèvre, Brie, Camembert," added M. Ritz.

"Not the Stones," said Ricky.

"Everything that matters," said Zenobia.

The rest of the day was spent in hectic preparation for the trip. Everyone packed and shopped and cleaned and visited the hairdresser and dry cleaner and travel agent. It was decided that they would fly across the Channel even though Zenobia made an urgent appeal to consider the train. She was still queasy from the airplane ride back from the Orient.

"We can't take the train," Ophelia

Ophelia prepares for the Trip

explained patiently, "because England is across the English Channel and trains do not go over water. We could take a boat but a plane is so much faster and the escalators at Charles de Gaulle Airport are such fun." Zenobia capitulated; she was secretly very fond of escalators.

Heidi and Clafouti, two very dear old friends of Ophelia's who spent most of their time encouraging young artists, graciously agreed to take care of the shop while everyone else was away.

After a sleepless night during which Ophelia tried on every white dress in her closet (eighty-three or eighty-seven, she lost count) to find exactly the right one for England—while Clarence assured her after each that it was perfect—Ophelia managed to pack three suitcases and a flight bag. Clarence took only a small satchel and an umbrella. Ricky Jaune carried a backpack and M. Ritz in his wooden carry-on cage. Conrad had a sturdy canvas case but it was very light because there was almost nothing

in it. "I prefer to bring things back," he explained. Zenobia brought several large ledgers to read on the flight and an overnight bag. "I can't see how I'll stay much longer," she insisted. "It's only for tea. Besides, I'm needed here."

"You're needed there too," advised Conrad. "I'm sure we all are. They can't possibly run the country properly without us."

"And what if we have an adventure or save a princess or win the Irish Sweepstakes?" suggested Ricky.

"I'm sure you can handle it without me," said Zenobia.

"I have plenty of clothes you can borrow," offered Ophelia, "and we can certainly buy whatever we need."

"And many things we don't," added Clarence.

With the luggage, it took two taxis to get the bears out to the airport. Zenobia set off the metal detector as they were entering the boarding area, but it turned out to be just her huge ring of keys to all the locks and cabinets and bureaus and drawers at Bazaar des Bears, and soon they were all settled on the airplane. The flight was short, no more than an hour, and the bears were disappointed that no breakfast was served. "This would never have happened on the train," remarked Zenobia. Fortunately, Clarence had packed a basket of croissants, *confitures*, and *jus de pamplemousse*, so no one was greatly indisposed.

As France dropped away off the wing of the plane, Zenobia looked out of the window and waved goodbye. There were so many places and countries in the world to see, so many marvelous cities and exciting people and wonderful adventures. But there was only one France. As delightful as it was to leave, she was only really happy coming home.

*Clarence, Ophelia,
Zenobia, Ricky,
Conrad, and
M. Ritz*

Ophelia's regal finery

II

It was a lovely, sunlit English afternoon when the bears reached London, which is to say it had only rained for half an hour from eleven A.M. on and off until noon. It was cold enough to wear your tweed jacket, a scarf, and a hat, but warm enough to carry your raincoat—except of course when it was raining— walk leisurely, and eat plenty of ice cream. The sun had poured down out of a cloud-speckled sky for at least a good five minutes at 11:30, 1:06, and two o'clock precisely. Altogether it was a truly delightful day to be in London.

In the three hours since arriving, the bears had checked into their hotel, seen Hyde Park, London Bridge, the Houses of Parliament, and Big Ben. They had done so much because when a bear puts his (her) mind to something it gets done. And that goes sixtuple for five bears and a mouse.

"There's Buckingham Palace," cried Ophelia. A stately columned temple rose before them like some magic city in a dream. A procession of brightly uniformed soldiers marched in front of the gates. It was the changing of the guard.

"How clever of the Queen to arrange for the army to meet us," said Ricky.

"They're here to arrest you," said Clarence. "They saw you steal that cake of soap from the plane."

"I needed it for later."

"Don't discourage the boy's hygiene," said Zenobia.

"The soldiers protect the Queen," Conrad explained. "She's a very important person. Even though she doesn't rule the country anymore, she's still very rich and powerful. She represents England to the whole world."

"Do you think we'll have chocolate cake?" asked Zenobia.

"I certainly hope so. I haven't come halfway around the world not to have chocolate cake," said Ricky Jaune.

"You have only come a few hundred miles," Conrad corrected. "And if the Queen of England serves fruitcake and cucumber sandwiches, I hope you will eat them and behave."

"I suppose so." Ricky sighed. "But it does seem a pity not to have at least chocolate biscuits or *mousse au chocolat* at Buckingham Palace."

It was 3:30 and everyone was terribly hungry. Clarence had suggested a light snack at a kiosk in the park or a *boîte* along the Thames, but Ophelia thought it would be terribly impolite of them to arrive at tea directly from lunch. And especially as the French begin lunch late, linger long, and conclude slowly, the bears decided to wait until tea. "Of course a *boîte* on the Thames wouldn't be the same as our *boîtes* along the Seine," observed Clarence.

But now at last they were walking down long, marbled halls lined with magnificent sculptures and priceless paintings.

"This place could really be brightened up with some cheerful chintzes and bits of silk from the shop," suggested Zenobia.

"We should send her our catalogue," said M. Ritz.

"But we don't have a catalogue," said Ophelia.

"There you go, my dear," added Clarence in his most soothing and reassuring voice. "A word to the wise."

"At least I have the Queen's order," said Ophelia, holding up a carefully wrapped parcel. "Every little bit helps."

As they passed room after room, each one large and splendidly decorated, the bears could not help but be impressed.

"Where do they find the time to fill them all?" asked Zenobia.

"They've been working on it for hundreds

of years," Clarence explained. "The building is used primarily for state functions or as a museum. Only a small part is lived in. We're coming to it now." And indeed, at the end of the hall was a door with a butler standing in front. He bowed and opened it onto a small, brightly lit room with warm pink curtains and overstuffed furniture. A large mahogany table was piled with silver urns, trays, and utensils and a huge platter heaped with mounds of cookies, cakes, biscuits, and sandwiches. In the very center, to everyone's immeasurable relief, was an immense wedge of gooey, sticky chocolate cake. The Queen was sitting in a simple wooden chair reading the *Times*. With a smile on her face like the equatorial sun, she rose, spread her arms, and gave Ophelia a big hug. Clarence, Conrad, Ricky, and M. Ritz bowed, Zenobia curtsied. The Queen pointed to a little table by her side.

"I wanted you to see it in all its glory," she said, beaming. It was the British royal crown with the pearl the bears had recovered in Japan fixed firmly in its place. Above the landscape of gilded tulle that formed the top of the crown, the pearl shone like the full moon over a still sea.

"It's too beautiful," said Ophelia.

Everyone was served double portions of cake and cookies with a few sandwiches on the side just to be sure. Then came the best part, the exchanging of gifts. Because the Queen was a queen, she went first. You could see how pleased and excited she was that she had found such fitting presents. There is nothing better than having a wonderful gift for somebody you truly love.

For Ophelia, the Queen had a tiny silver mirror engraved with the words "Dieu et Mon Droit" which was the motto of the coat of arms of England. It was in French so Ophelia knew it meant "God and my right."

"Why is the motto of England in French?" asked Ricky of Clarence in a polite whisper.

"Because long ago the kings of England came over from Normandy in France. For many hundreds of years all the nobles in the English court spoke French," Clarence whispered back.

Next the Queen gave Zenobia a gold pen and pencil set and, for Ricky, a silver box to keep his glasses in. For Conrad, she had a pair of deerskin gloves dyed a bright red, and for Clarence, a large leather portfolio to keep his notes and restaurant reviews in. The presents were perfect and it was clear that the Queen had thought long and hard about each one. Then the bears brought out their gifts.

Ophelia produced an exquisite lacquer tea set from her trip to Japan. Since the Queen served so much tea, Ophelia knew that another set would certainly come in handy. Indeed, the Queen was delighted and said that she had never seen such beautiful designs. Zenobia gave the Queen a pink silk nightcap for those long cold English winter nights. Ricky Jaune had brought a pair of bright green sunglasses in the Queen's own size, and Clarence had a collection of all his reviews and articles bound in leather and inscribed "To the Queen of good taste, with much love, Clarence." But the best gift of all was from Conrad, who had designed a box to look like a miniature Buckingham Palace. And in front of it, marching in step, was a whole troop of tiny bear soldiers made out of lead. The Queen was utterly charmed and hugged Conrad twice. She promised to put them in her bedroom and let only her very closest friends and grandchildren play with them. M. Ritz even had a gift for the Queen's dog: a lovely ball with golden ribbons.

Now it was time for more food and tea. When it looked for a terrible moment as if they might run out of cake, a servant instantly appeared with a new one. After a really wonderful breakfast, there is no better meal than tea! Actually, many people prefer tea to breakfast because at tea there is absolutely no need to eat anything that is good for you. Bears love tea. Of course, bears frequently eat that sort of thing for breakfast as well—but only if they've been very good about dinner the night before. Bears are very good about dinner.

"How I love Paris," said the Queen. "I miss it so."

"One is only truly alive in Paris," Ophelia added.

"How true," Zenobia agreed.

"But London is certainly an exciting place," Ricky volunteered. "I love all the girls in shocking pink. Where do you go for bow ties?"

Alfred, the Queen's dog©

"I don't require a large selection," the Queen confessed with perhaps a trace of sadness. "I've heard that the best ones come from a fabric store called Liberty of London. You should look there if you can. And Turnbull & Asser is also nice."

"I was hoping to find a good solid croquet set to take back home. Do you have any suggestions?" Conrad inquired.

"Go to Harrods. They have everything. Of course, if you want the best, then go to Asprey's. But you'd better bring lots of pounds," the Queen replied. "Tons."

"No price is too high for a good game of croquet," Conrad said emphatically.

"Where are you going after London?" the Queen asked.

"We were hoping to see something of the country," answered Clarence.

"We hear the Lake District where all the Romantic poets lived and wrote is very beautiful," observed Ophelia. "I'm an incurable romantic. And perhaps a frustrated poet too."

"We are all frustrated poets," the Queen agreed. "All who love beauty are poets."

"And underpaid," Conrad muttered. His last two operas had done poorly and he was frequently not given full wages if the show failed to make a profit. Such was the life of the artist.

Suddenly a loud cry was heard from the far end of the hall. Everyone turned to see a distinguished figure in formal attire with a brightly striped sash running toward them. It was Albert Hanover, a distant relative of the Queen, in town to do research at the Tate Gallery. He had stopped at the palace

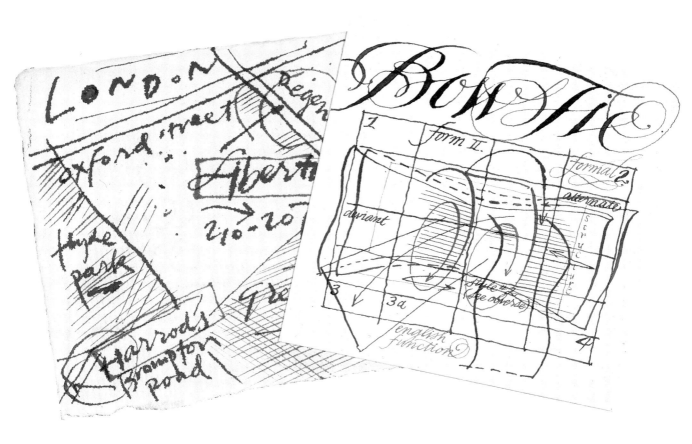

The Queen's
sumptuous
Spread

to take a nap and had recognized his old friend Ophelia from across a half-mile-long hall. "I'd know that nose anywhere," chuckled Albert, rushing over to give her a big hug. "You look magnificent."

"Didn't I sell you that piece of silk?" asked Ophelia, indicating the red stripe across Albert's chest.

"I bought enough to wrap my whole family and the next seventy generations of Hanovers." Albert laughed. "Where are you staying? How long are you going to be in England?"

"We're just here for a day or two," said Zenobia. "We really have to get back."

"No we don't," squeaked M. Ritz.

"I've just received an urgent telegram from Dr. Ernest Churchill. He's made a critical breakthrough in the training of his butterfly hound, Papillon. The dog can now run at full speed looking up. We must all go out to Bruinyes House immediately. I'm leaving tonight. You must come. It was the only thing that could have kept him from tea."

"Dear Ernie, such a wonderful bear," sighed the Queen. "How unfortunate . . ."

Albert looked odd. Ophelia was puzzled. "Is something wrong with Dr. Churchill?" she asked.

"I really shouldn't say," the Queen replied. "It's only a rumor."

"It's not even a rumor," Albert volunteered. "It's a possibility."

"How dreadful," said Ophelia. "I hope it's nothing concerning Aunt Vita."

"Please tell us," huffed Clarence. "We're beginning to be worried."

"There are problems at Bruinyes House," whispered the Queen. "I think you should go there. Poor Ernie desperately needs your help."

"I would like to know what's wrong," Ricky complained.

"It's probably nothing," the Queen said firmly. "You know how stories are exaggerated in the country."

"I'll tell you all about it tonight," Albert said hastily. "We'll have dinner at the Connaught. I must pick up Anemone. Then we'll catch the last train to Sissinghurst. Dr. Churchill will be so happy to see you. Aunt Vita will be in heaven."

"Sissinghurst!" exclaimed Zenobia. "We can't possibly go to Sissinghurst."

"Of course we can," said Ophelia, Clarence, Conrad, and Ricky Jaune. "Ernie needs us."

"But why?" asked M. Ritz.

"I'll tell you at dinner," said Albert. "Six at the Connaught."

"I couldn't possibly," said Zenobia.

"We may be a little late," Ophelia conceded.

"Six-thirty then," Albert proposed. "But I won't take no for an answer."

"I hope I won't set off the metal detector again," moaned Zenobia.

"There are no metal detectors in train stations," explained Conrad.

"Thank heaven for small favors," sighed Zenobia.

Conrad's gift to the Queen

In the reading room of the British Museum Library

III

A TRIP TO THE COUNTRY

After a hectic afternoon making last-minute purchases for their trip to the country, the bears paid a quick visit to the British Museum Library for something to read on the train. There were thirty-four million books to choose from and nobody was having an easy time making a decision, Ophelia least of all.

Finally she selected *Mrs. Beeton's Book of Household Management*. Clarence opted for the *Universal Encyclopaedia of Trifles*. M. Ritz had *The Love of Cheese*. Conrad had *Wagner Made Hard* (in the original German), and Zenobia was deciding between the complete Shakespeare or the collected Shaw.

"But they're three thousand pages each. You'll never finish them on the train," said Ophelia.

"They're certainly impressive volumes," said Clarence with new respect. "I didn't know you were so literary."

"I'm improving myself," she answered.

"I'm improving myself, too," said Ricky, holding up his book: *Mastering the Art of Hang-Gliding*.

"Not from my roof, you don't," Ophelia admonished. "If you want to fly one of those things, take it to the Eiffel Tower."

"They won't let you," said Conrad.

"You could always fly it up," suggested M. Ritz, "and take the elevator down."

"Excuse me," said the head librarian, coming over to Clarence. "We've put your name through the computer and it seems you already have one of our books out: *A Moveable Feast* by Hemingway."

"That was such a wonderful book, all about Paris," mused Clarence fondly. "Are you sure I didn't return it?"

"I'm sorry. Our records show you've never brought it back. It's a few years overdue," said the librarian.

"A few years overdue!" exclaimed Conrad. "Clarence, *vous êtes méchant*. You wicked boy."

"I must have taken it home after the Coronation. I promise I'll send it back as soon as I can," said Clarence, deeply chagrined.

"That's quite all right. We're so glad you enjoyed it. Come by anytime," said the librarian.

At 6:35 the bears entered the elaborately wood-paneled and mirrored bar of the Connaught Hotel. Zenobia was reconciled to yet another of Ophelia's wonderful adventures and beginning to enjoy herself. Wisps of cigar smoke swirled and drifted up into the high-raftered ceiling and hung like a thin cloud at the edges of the room. Albert commanded a huge table in the center at which was seated a tall thin bear bundled up to her ears in an elegant red silk brocade coat. Albert stood up as the bears approached and bowed to each one, who bowed back and kissed Anemone's hand. Anemone was the bewitching exotic dancer with the Ballet Russe for whom Albert had given up the

id="2" />

Dinner at the Connaught with Albert and Anemone

throne. "Nijinsky dreamed of dancing with her," Albert confided in a low voice to Ophelia. "But whenever she was in Monte Carlo, he was in Moscow. And when she was in Moscow, he was in Monte Carlo. So tragic."

Ricky Jaune had on a green striped bow tie. "From Liberty of London," he said proudly. Conrad wore his new gloves. Hot chocolate was ordered and plates and canapés appeared. A pleasant background hum of British accents and laughter enveloped the table. It was just like being in someone's very large, very comfy, very warm living room.

"I spoke to Dr. Churchill on the phone. He's ecstatic that you're coming," said Albert. "Papillon is ready for his first full-scale test. It should take place early tomorrow morning and I told him we'd be there. But it's time I confessed: all is not well at Bruinyes House."

"How not well?" asked Conrad. "A slight rheum, or full-scale physical discombobulation?"

"I don't think it's as bad as all that," Albert reassured. "There have been strange occurrences. Lights go on all through the house at odd hours and in strange places. Music echoes down the halls. Messages appear on windows and in mirrors. I suspect there are vandals in the area. Or maybe Ernie is so preoccupied with his research he's becoming forgetful. I'm sure there's no truth to the rumor that it's haunted."

"Haunted!" Zenobia cried in disbelief. "Who would believe such a ridiculous idea."

"There *is* local folklore about a spirit inhabiting Bruinyes House," Albert told the startled bears, "but nobody puts much stock in those old stories anymore."

"What kind of stories?" Clarence asked, with a worried glance at Ricky, who seemed to be growing more trepidant with every word Albert uttered.

"I'm not the least bit scared," exclaimed M. Ritz, who had chased more than his share of tough cats from Bazaar des Bears.

"There is a legend that Sir Henry Bruinyes, an irascible old sea captain, swore that no ship of his would ever sink," continued Albert. "He built Bruinyes House to be the most splendid mansion of its day. It was reefed and trimmed with the most exquisite appointments—mahogany furniture, silver fixtures, silk and satin for all the curtains and cushions. It was a rare vessel indeed. But it has sunk."

"How can a house sink?" asked Ricky.

"A house can go down as surely as a four-masted schooner if the crew neglects it," Albert explained. "I wouldn't be surprised if old Henry is back, howling for blood."

"How terrifying," shivered Zenobia.

"Dr. Churchill wouldn't invite us down if there were any real danger," affirmed Clarence. "And certainly Aunt Vita wouldn't tolerate anything of the sort. I'm sure if there's anything wrong we can help solve the problem."

"Certainly Ophelia can," said Conrad.

"I don't believe in ghosts," whispered Anemone.

"Neither do I," added Ophelia.

Dr. Churchill and Albert with Papillon

The mistress of the manor,
Aunt Vita

"Ernie thinks it's just squirrels in the attic," agreed Albert. "I hope he's right."

"I don't like the sound of this at all," Ricky muttered.

"*I* think it sounds like a real adventure," exclaimed Conrad. "When do we leave?"

"After dinner. What's your pleasure? I recommend the sole," said Albert, perusing the menu with a serious eye. "But then, of course, the Scotch salmon . . ."

It was salmon all around with truffles and trifles and hot chocolate with whipped cream and strawberries and cream and tea

with cream and more chocolate cake and chocolate mousse with whipped cream and chocolate mousse cake (clotted cream optional) and peaches and cream and berries and cream and hot chocolate and double cream. England was famous for its dairy industry and almost everything was served with cream. Ophelia was truly happy. "I must remember to remember what you serve with cream. I've clearly missed any number of opportunities."

"It's always best to serve cream first and

worry about the protocol later," said Albert. "That's what the British do."

"Very wise," Clarence agreed.

Soon it was time to go. They stopped by the hotel to pick up the luggage, then off to Victoria Station. Albert had reserved a large compartment so that everyone could sit together, but there were very few people on the train. Some overzealous partyers were nodding dreamily over their seats; a businessman or two forced to put in extra hours read through last-minute notes and reports on the way home.

Trains were still the best way to go to and from London, even for many who had cars. Ophelia took a little nap on Clarence's shoulder. It had been an awfully long day. Zenobia nodded with her head bumping against the window. Albert and Anemone whispered quietly to each other. Conrad looked out at the passing lights of the houses and farms.

Ricky, however, was wide awake. There was no one to talk to and his head was filled with thoughts of angry sea captains guarding their booty. He tried to read his book, then he tried to read Ophelia's book, then Clarence's book. Then he tried to tie his bow ties together. Then he folded a piece of newspaper into a boat. Then he wrote a poem to the Queen in honor of her chocolate cake. At last he got up and walked slowly through the train to see who was there.

In the first car, everyone was asleep. In the second car, everyone was asleep or playing cards. In the third car, a small boy was playing with a toy plane while his mother read a big, thick book with a purple cover and the words "Love, Passion, Greed, Ecstasy" on the cover, more or less in that order, though Ricky could not be sure.

At the end of the third car, Ricky noticed

ODE TO THE QUEEN'S CAKE
—
BY RICKY JAUNE
—

O, Chocolate Cake,
    O, dark, O, light
O Cake, my favorite
        thing to bite
O, fudge, O phooey
    O, sticky, O, gooey
So soft, so sweet
    So now let's eat
—

a row of green spikes protruding over the
top of one of the seats. It looked like a line
of small asparagus shoots growing from the
edge of the vinyl. How curious that asparagus should grow in a train, thought Ricky, I
wonder how it tastes. He walked up to the
seat and saw that the seedlings were con-
nected to a ball of beige fur. It was a head
with hair cut, braided, and dyed into green
rows. The head was attached to a body
laced into a tight black leather jacket and
pants. Ricky looked at this apparition quite
amazed and uncertain. Was it alive?

The creature returned his gaze. It smiled
at him. One tooth was colored green to
match the hair. "I've been waiting for you,"
the creature said and extended a paw
toward Ricky. Ricky stood immobile until
the paw (it seemed to take forever) finally
touched him, then he turned and ran for
dear life down all three cars. He leapt for
Ophelia's arms, shouting loud enough to
wake the world for twenty miles around,
"Save me! Help! It's after me!" And as
much as Ophelia, Zenobia, Conrad, Clarence, Alfred, Anemone, and M. Ritz
pleaded and begged, Ricky would not say a
word about it.

Dr. Churchill was waiting for them when they disembarked. Of course Albert had told him when they were leaving so he knew when they'd arrive. Trains are always on time in England. Dr. Churchill gave everybody a hug, and the bears were so happy to see him again. It had been just a little while since they were all together in Japan, but even a short separation is painful for true friends. He was wearing a huge assortment of medals in honor of the visit of so many of his Parisian *confrères*. It was a very short drive to Bruinyes House and everyone was much too tired to pay attention to the beautiful tall trees and the broad clear streams and the low rolling hills which are so typical of the English countryside.

"I just want to sleep," said Ophelia.

"Me too," said Zenobia, Conrad, Clarence, Alfred, Anemone, and M. Ritz.

"Save me. Help. It's after me," whimpered Ricky Jaune.

"Is there something I can do?" asked Dr. Churchill.

"Not at the moment," explained Ophelia. "Maybe tomorrow."

In the morning, after a long, restful sleep there was a long breakfast presided over by Aunt Vita, the somewhat eccentric but indomitable mistress of Bruinyes House. In her spare time Vita made hats for all the neighbors, and on her own head was an immense bonnet of pink felt and black silk ribbons. "Would you like to see the place?" she offered. "I don't think you've ever been here, my dear," she said affectionately to Ophelia. "Or have you?" Vita's memory often skipped around from yesterday to the Gay Nineties to the Roaring Twenties and back.

"We want to see the ghost," said M. Ritz.

"Ghost! Balderdash and piffle,"

exclaimed Aunt Vita. "Absolutely without foundation," confirmed Dr. Churchill. "There's an owl in the attic, bats in the belfry, squirrels in the sitting room. This is an old house and it's seen better days. Far better days." Vita sighed. "I'll show you." She marched them from top to bottom, room by room, through every corner, crevice, and cranny. It was a sorry sight.

The furniture was covered with dustcloths, the floors were covered with waves and eddies of dust, rivers of dust ran through the halls, along the walls, up the stairs, and down the corridors. Mirrors were blotted with the gray accumulation of the years. Pictures were indecipherable. Chandeliers dangled thin streamers of cobwebs. Little hills and valleys of gray and white lay on the tables and bureaus. Here and there the ceiling poked up through the floor and the floor poked down through the ceiling.

"Heavens," said Ophelia. "What happened?"

"Neglect and taxes, an ineluctable combination," sighed Dr. Churchill.

"I believe it," said Ricky.

"You don't even know what that means," said Zenobia.

"I see what it is," he replied.

"We all do," said Clarence. "The real question is what can be done."

"We've tried opening the house to tourists once a week," explained Dr. Churchill.

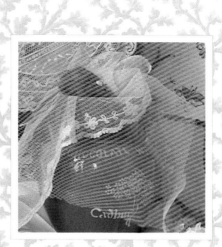

Bruinjes House's
dusty drapes and
covered furniture

"Black Wednesday," groaned Aunt Vita.

"We're not precisely delighted with our local tourists. The money isn't nearly enough and they tramp through the rooms like elephants."

"Send them to us," Zenobia volunteered. "We'll put up a big sign at the gate: Bazaar des Bears, 327 miles, next right."

"There must be something we can do," declared Ophelia. "Surely a house like this was a part of English history. There must be some remarkable event or personage you could advertise to attract customers?"

"Maybe somebody famous like Winnie-the-Pooh once slept here," said Zenobia.

"Or William the Conqueror," volunteered Albert.

"Or Caruso," Conrad suggested.

"Or Ringo," Ricky offered.

"That would improve our attendance," Dr. Churchill agreed. "But I don't think we can establish it with any certainty. That nonsensical blather about spirits or spooks hasn't helped matters either."

"We could lie," said Ricky tentatively.

"Ricky!" exclaimed Clarence.

"Well, that's just modern salesmanship. You don't really lie, you embellish," the boy explained. "It's a science."

"He's right, you know, that's how it's done in the newspapers," said Conrad. "That's how we sell tickets to *Aida*."

"Not *Aida*!" cried Anemone.

"Alas," sighed Conrad. "Even *Aida*."

"We have to think of something honest," said Ophelia. "Certainly we can come up with something. We are, after all, bears!" And the gloom that had slowly settled over everyone instantly began to disperse. Once Ophelia made up her mind, it was as good as done—no problem too large, no conundrum too convoluted, no dilemma too daunting.

"I have a feeling this is going to involve work," sighed Ricky.

"Of course it is," said M. Ritz.

"This was supposed to be a vacation," Ricky moaned.

"Your life is a vacation, young man," Conrad interjected.

"This is a good deed," added Albert. "If we can save Bruinyes House, the Queen herself would be grateful."

"Wonderful," said Ricky. "Good deeds are work. Vacations are work. My life is work. Maybe we can have a disaster and I'll get some time off."

Aunt Vita and Zenobia assess the situation

Papillon, with Dr. Churchill and W. Ritz

IV

While Ophelia was thinking, Dr. Churchill made preparations for the first scientifically documented test of Papillon, the hound he had been training for five years to distinguish butterflies by their smell. "First, I taught him to recognize elephants, then giraffes, then large musk oxen, then zebras. Then llamas, boar, sheep, raccoons, rabbits, squirrels, pigeons, grouse, frogs, lizards, hummingbirds, dragonflies, and at last butterflies—the gray, beige, ochre, and mocha and salmon colored ones first, then maroon, fuchsia, puce, and almond, and finally emerald, lilac, orange, and blue. It's been exhausting," Dr. Churchill complained.

"I worked ten years on my tour jeté," Anemone confided. "All really significant achievements in life take time."

"Too true," agreed Ophelia. "Bazaar des Bears was not built in a day."

"Now we are ready," said Dr. Churchill. "This is the moment I've lived for."

"It certainly is historic," said Albert. "Do you think we should have a photographer?"

"If this is successful we won't need a photographer. It will be on the front pages of all the newspapers all around the world," said Dr. Churchill.

"How can it be on the front page of all the newspapers if we don't have a photographer to take a picture?" asked Ophelia.

But Dr. Churchill was already busy positioning the dog at the top of the hill. The bears waited in the valley below. It was a broad field dotted with wild flowers. Millions of butterflies of every conceivable color and shape danced and fluttered from bloom to bloom. Dr. Churchill held up a particularly rare blue spotted anaximander to Papillon's nose. It was a species found on only one form of pale purple salpiglossis on sunny late June mornings. It was a critical test, and the dog would have his paws full succeeding. Nevertheless Dr. Churchill was hopeful. "No use wasting any more time. Off you go, Papillon. Yoicks!" cried Dr. Churchill.

The dog bounded off, its nose straight up in the air, its eyes pointed to the sky on the trail of the elusive prey. The bears cheered and hullooed. There is no greater inspiration to a hero in pursuit of a noble cause than the hulloo of a pack of bears. Papillon ran for all he was worth, back and forth, up and down, high and low through the fields. In the warm summer distance the majestic sagging bulk of Bruinyes House simmered and swam. Butterflies cavorted through the air. Papillon sniffed at every one, searching for the precise essence. He smelled a thousand butterflies, two thousand, fifteen thousand. His nose was wet and quivering. What if there were no spotted anaximanders to be found? What if all the pale purple salpiglossis—a particularly surly flower if there ever was one—had chosen to grow in the fields half a mile down the road? Would the test be a failure?

Suddenly there was a tremendous bark. Dr. Churchill came running, the bears following close behind. Papillon was leaping and bouncing like an acrobat. On top of a fragile crimson flower a magnificent streak of blue tissue hovered in the air. It was the anaximander. Papillon was delirious. Dr. Churchill was delirious. Ophelia was hugging Zenobia and Aunt Vita. Clarence was hugging Conrad and Ricky. Albert was hugging Anemone. M. Ritz was doing somersaults. And from out of the house like some eerie enchanted hymn there came the rich plangent sound of an accordion playing a perfect rendition of "The Roses of Picardy."

Everyone congratulated Dr. Churchill and patted him on the back. Papillon got big hugs and kisses from Zenobia, Anemone, and Ophelia. Albert declared the day a national holiday and called up the *Times* to

notify the rest of England. Clarence made preparations for a chocolate cake party— five different kinds of chocolate cake: chocolate cake with chocolate frosting, white cake with chocolate frosting, chocolate cake with white frosting, chocolate chip cake with chocolate frosting, and white cake with chocolate chip frosting (with hot chocolate to drink and all the napkins folded into different shapes—swans, planes, flowers, boats, and trumpets).

Ricky asked, "Who's playing the accordion?"

"Aunt Vita is," replied Dr. Churchill.

"No, I'm not," answered Aunt Vita from the other end of the kitchen where she was making punch.

"It's Conrad," said Clarence.

"Conrad was with us outside," observed M. Ritz, "when the music began. And Conrad doesn't play the accordion."

"He could have learned," said Zenobia.

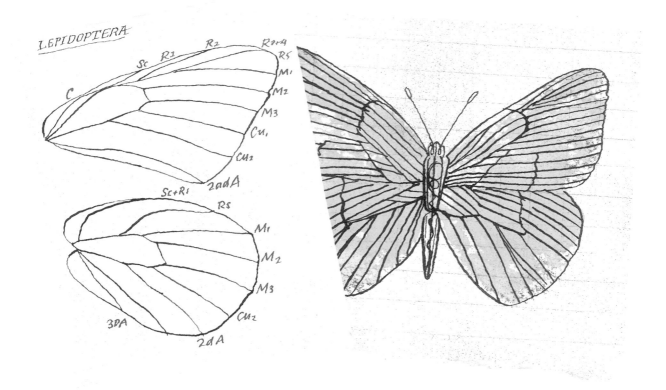

Ricky Jaune and Zenobia Onassis

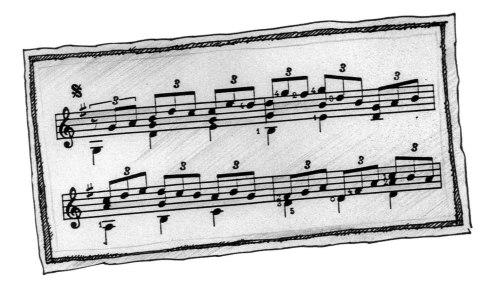

"Conrad could learn anything."

"Even if he learned, he still couldn't play the accordion from the house while he was outside with us. You just can't learn that sort of thing," Ophelia remarked.

"Conrad could," said Zenobia.

"Something very strange is going on," said Ophelia. "Where do you keep the accordion, Ernie?"

"We don't have an accordion," noted Dr. Churchill.

The warm, melodic harmonies of the accordion echoed and reverberated throughout the house.

"Then it must be wind in the attics," said Dr. Churchill.

"I'm going upstairs to look," said Ophelia.

"I'll go with you," Clarence volunteered, as did Conrad.

"Me too," said Zenobia.

"And me," said Ricky Jaune, sticking close to the others.

"I'll show you the way," Dr. Churchill declared.

The bears set off up the stairs like spelunkers, cave explorers following the murky paths and twisting tunnels of an unknown space, tapping at the walls to see, by how the sounds reverberate, how solid the stone was. But instead of tapping, the music boomed and hummed, leading them on. They went from level to level, peering around corners and down corridors, expecting at any moment to come face to face with heaven knows what.

"I think I'm getting scared," whispered Ricky.

"I've been scared for over an hour," admitted Clarence.

"Do you think it's Sir Henry?" Ricky asked tremulously.

At every step the floors creaked, a flurry of dust seemed to attack, the music seemed to emanate from a different direction.

"We could turn back," suggested Conrad, looking about nervously.

"We're at the top of the house," said Dr. Churchill, coming to a final landing with just a shaky railing visible, leading up to the roof. "See, I told you there was nothing." The music continued to play, louder than ever. It was so strong that it seemed almost to be coming from inside everyone's head.

"I think he's right," agreed Ricky. "Nothing. Let's go back."

"Clearly it's squirrels," added Conrad.

Ophelia stooped to pick up a piece of bright, translucent color. She shook off the dust and held a luminous piece of multicolored fabric in her paw.

"This is exquisite," gasped Ophelia. "Where did it come from?"

"Sir Henry Bruinyes sailed all over the world and brought back curiosities from everyplace he went," explained Dr. Churchill. "Nothing very valuable, alas, but charming knickknacks from Spain, France, Holland, the South Seas, America, China, Japan. Heaven knows where this came

from. I didn't know any of it had survived."

"Wherever it came from," Ophelia cheered, "it's gorgeous and a lot more valuable than you think."

"Really?" exclaimed Dr. Churchill. "Who would have thought?"

"Could there be more where this came from?" asked Zenobia. "Behind that door?" She pointed up.

"It's possible. I've never been there myself," admitted Dr. Churchill. "The stairway goes to the roof, I think. But you never know."

"Could we see?" asked Ophelia. "Look! there's another ribbon." Indeed, scattered along the rickety planking of a narrow catwalk, a dusty trail of ribbons led up to the tiny wood door. Carefully the bears proceeded up the steps. Dr. Churchill pushed against the door, which gave way with a sullen creak. They were not on the roof but inside a large, cluttered dust-filled attic.

"I'm absolutely amazed," gasped Dr. Churchill. "I never dreamed this was here."

Strange
occurrences in
the attic

The accordion music swooped and soared in triumph though still with no accordion or accordion player visible.

"This is just like a fairy tale," exclaimed Conrad. "The secret room at the top where Rumpelstiltskin weaves straw into gold."

"I don't see any straw," said Ricky. "Though there's certainly a lot of everything else."

"Ophelia! Look at this exquisite fabric," cried Zenobia, holding up a length of gold damask lawn. "It's worth a fortune. We could sell this in Paris for a thousand francs."

"This garret looks just like my workroom at La Scala," Conrad admitted. "We have as much cloth as this and I won't tell you what we pay for it."

All thoughts of ghostly music fled from their minds as the bears gaped at the huge assemblage of goods. There were bolts of silk in red, green, yellow, blue, black, and a design called ancient madder which was swirls of all of these colors that twisted and spun together like a rainbow whirlwind. There were trunks of Spanish lace, English velvet, and French brocade, crepe de chine as thin as a butterfly's wing and wool as thick as a slice of beef. From one box, particolored ribbons cascaded out for yards over the surrounding floor. In another, a huge nest of scarves in soft pastels coiled and squirmed.

"This is a treasure trove," Ophelia gasped.

"Can you really put a price on this old cave of rags?" asked Dr. Churchill.

"The curtains belonged to the Ribbon King," said Clarence, pointing to a mass of tangled fabric.

"Really? Are you sure? How do you know?" asked Dr. Churchill.

"It says so on the mirror," explained Clarence, gesturing at a large, ornate gilt mirror with that exact message written in the dust on the glass.

"Ricky, stop finger-painting," said Zenobia. "This is serious."

"I didn't do a thing," replied Ricky in a huff.

"The curtains are exquisite," Conrad observed. "Perhaps I could sell them to the Paris Opéra."

"There was a rumor," muttered Dr. Churchill, "that Sir Henry was a pirate. Any number of these could have been stolen on the high seas."

"Or off the low roads," said Conrad, fingering a particularly gaudy cloth, "if purple twills are any indication."

"I think we can make something of all this," said Ophelia, thinking out loud.

"Most of it's awfully tattered," Zenobia remarked.

"We'd have to cut the edges off and the worn parts, but the rest is superb. It's priceless."

"Many houses in this part of England have attics full of old fabric," Dr. Churchill noted. "Is it really so special?"

"It's what you do with it that matters," advised Ophelia. "We can combine these antique fabrics with fresh material and find imaginative uses for them—for instance, patchwork spreads or pillowcases, handkerchiefs, tablecloths, napkins, sachets. We can tie the ribbons on dresses or as sashes on hats. It would be lovely. People would come from all over England to buy them."

"It sounds like Bazaar des Bears of Britain," exclaimed Clarence.

"That would be wonderful," cheered Dr. Churchill. "But who would make the stock and who would sell it?"

"Why you and Aunt Vita, of course," said Clarence, "or any of the local people could be trained to run a store right here in Bruinyes House. It would attract lots more tourists."

"And with all those people coming through to look and buy, you could open up a restaurant," added Ophelia. "I could give you my recipe for lemonade."

"And mine for chocolate cake," chimed Clarence.

"This is too exciting," said Dr. Churchill. "I don't know where to begin."

"We should begin right here. This will be our factory. Zenobia and I will clean and trim the fabric, sew the pieces together, make the goods that Clarence, Conrad, and Anemone can sell downstairs. If you can find us one or two people to help whom we can train to run the operation, we'll be all set," said Ophelia.

"There are several wonderful ladies who used to work for Bruinyes House in more

prosperous days," Dr. Churchill thought aloud. "I'm sure they'd love to come back."

"I feel as if I'm here at the creation of a new country or a great moment in history," said Ricky. "Do you think I'll get my portrait on the wall?"

"With or without your hang-glider?" sighed Conrad.

"Why is this ribbon hanging in the middle of the air?" observed Zenobia.

"Spider webs," said Dr. Churchill and passed his hand above the floating bit of fabric, which promptly fell to the floor.

"When do we start?" asked Ernie.

"Right away," said Ophelia. "That is, right after lunch."

Lunch in the conservatory

V

CLEANING UP
THE PAST

Lunch was in the conservatory, a lovely plant- and flower-filled room with a wall of glass from floor to ceiling to let in the light. There was a view toward the downs, soft pillowy hills threaded with fuzzy trees and gauzy bushes. Off at the edge of sight, a thin blue river bumped among the ruins of old stone barns, weathered barrows and abandoned churches overgrown with weeds.

Neither the scenery nor the curious events of the morning had diminished the bears' appetites. First they were served a soup course, split pea with lentils, then a salad with cheese and toasted bread crumbs and anchovies, then an omelet with vegetables, then sausages with biscuits and muffins, then fried fish, then fruit and raspberry sherbet, then of course Clarence's cakes and hot chocolate with double cream. Even Ricky was full. After all, this was only lunch and just a few hours before tea. But lunch is a very important meal in England and an even more important meal in France. So when very hungry bears from France are in England, lunch is taken very seriously.

"I've called up everybody I could think of," Dr. Churchill informed them all as they sat around waiting for lunch to settle. "Edwina and Freddy, the old chambermaid and butler, are definitely coming. And we possibly might have volunteers from the Croquet Society, the Women's Sewing Circle, the Association for Needy Mahogany, and the Light Arms and Drilling Team. I figured the more the merrier, as we say in England."

"Excellent," said Aunt Vita. "There's so much that needs to be done. Why, we can use everyone, if only to clean the dust."

"There's so much dust here. You really don't know what's dirty or simply a whole new kind of dust architecture," said Albert.

"You English love dust. You're not happy unless there's at least ten years of dust on anything," added Conrad.

"Anything with less than ten is really not suitable for human utilization," conceded Dr. Churchill. "But over thirty-five, you tend to forget what the bloody thing is."

"A little dust does wonders for most everything," Ophelia mused. "I'm loath to overdust. But it's certainly true that Bruinyes House could use a thorough cleaning. Why don't we go all the way and turn this mansion upside down, pull off the dustcloths, dust the tables and mirrors, clean and wax the floors, beat the rugs, clean the furniture, polish the silver. Once the money starts coming in you can do the major repairs, but there's an awful lot we can do right now. Especially if we all work hard and there are enough volunteers."

"What a lovely idea," cheered Aunt Vita. "This was such a beautiful house long ago. I remember the parties. Hundreds of dashing young men in full military regalia, sabers flashing, medals by the dozens. And women

in silk and brocade dancing like dervishes. It makes my heart sing."

"I remember the balls at the Czar's palace in St. Petersburg. All of Russia was there. The men were so tall, the women slender and frail like fairies," Anemone whispered.

"Not you," exclaimed Albert, "my ice princess. You were a polar bear."

"I still am," Anemone laughed, "and you are my robber prince."

The doorbell rang. With much fanfare, Dr. Churchill let in two very British-looking bears. "You flew," he exclaimed. "These are Edwina and Freddy whom I told you about. They're priceless."

Edwina was a small, cheerful bear in a blue cotton dress. Freddy stood next to her straight as a new chimney.

Edwina curtsied to all the ladies. "I used to be the upstairs chambermaid," she explained to Ophelia. "Or was it the downstairs chambermaid? The upstairs chambermaid. Yes, I'm sure. Unless it was the downstairs chambermaid? No, no, no. Well, I want to help."

"And I want to help too," said Freddy.

"We both want to help. We love this house. We'll do anything we can," said Edwina.

"You're so kind," Ophelia replied.

"There's so much to do, but with friends like you, Bruinyes House will soon be shining again."

Ophelia set everyone to work. Conrad, Aunt Vita, and Ricky began on the living room. Zenobia, Anemone, and Edwina went up into the attic to catalogue all the goods, pile them against the walls, and make room for sewing machines and work tables. Clarence, Dr. Churchill, Albert, and Freddy moved the furniture outside to be cleaned and aired. Ophelia went from room to room assigning the tasks to be done (with M. Ritz to protect her from the dust devils), making plans and thinking of ways to restore faded curtains, cabinets, cushions, and antimacassars to pristine splendor. All day long volunteers kept arriving, adding to the roster of Ophelia's army. By evening, Bruinyes House looked like a small city with people scurrying every which way, up and down halls, across lawns, carrying sofas out, moving tables up and around, waxing, polishing, scrubbing, dusting, wiping, drying, straightening, taking down and putting back up. And gradually, room by room, the place began to look elegant. The mahogany shone, the silver sparkled. Old, faded colors glowed in the luminous air now that the mediating layers of dust and dirt had been swept away.

"Now I see what Vita and Ernie were talking about," confessed Conrad. "I didn't really believe this old barn could ever have equaled a decent chateau in the Loire. Now I think it's just as good. Well, almost."

"Perhaps," Clarence agreed, "but the wine cellar is scandalous. I can't give a house four stars without a solid wine cellar."

Meanwhile, Ophelia had closeted herself in the attic. She sat before her sewing machine, a huge basket of material on one side, Papillon nestled in a heap on the other. Slowly at first, then with increasing confi-

Freddy and Edwina, loyal retainers

Ophelia's inspiration

dence, she cut bits of fabric from the bolts and pieced them together, making larger and larger swatches of patchwork. These in turn were stitched together to make handbags, pillowcases, capes, skirts, shirts, sachets, pillows, belts, potholders, tea cozies; all the elegant finery for which Bazaar des Bears is famous. Edwina watched carefully and was soon as quick, nimble, and creative as Ophelia herself or, well, Zenobia. As each item was finished, Ophelia added one of the beautiful ribbons along an edge or strap or collar to give it that extraspecial appeal. Ophelia was so absorbed in her task she barely noticed that often as she reached for a ribbon, it would be floating in the air in front of her. Sometimes as she finished a garment, unseen hands would lift it off the table and pile it magically in the appropriate place. Only Edwina noted the curious life which inanimate objects seemed to possess in Bruinyes House.

"Excuse me, ma'am," Edwina interjected. "Have you ever heard of Sir Henry's ghost?"

"Albert mentioned something about it," answered Ophelia. "But it seems rather speculative."

"It wasn't speculative to Captain Brademas who sailed the good ship *Darkside* in 1797. It was positively unhealthy," Edwina whispered.

"I can't say I put much stock in fairy tales," confessed Ophelia. "But I do enjoy a good story."

"This was a classic, ma'am, if I say so myself," began Edwina. "Old Josiah Brademas sailed 'round the world four times with Sir Henry and each time made such a ruckus, nagging and complaining, Sir Henry swore he'd never let that bear set foot on his ship again. Well, Brademas retired from active duty and took up the leisured life in the country, hunting and fishing and carousing in taverns. Sir Henry figured that was fine as long as the Captain kept to his side of the island. Pretty much he did, and in time drinking and carousing got the better of the Captain. He died and was buried in his old sea chest in the woods of Lincolnshire, and Sir Henry died and was buried in Sissinghurst. Everything was as fine as you could wish it; but strange as these things may be, the woods of Lincolnshire were turned into housing projects, and one of Josiah's daughters married one of Sir Henry's sons, and someone thought it might be nice if the Captain's bones rested here near Sir Henry's. So sure enough, the sea chest with Brademas was moved across half of England, up roads and down rivers on its way to the Sissinghurst Our Lady of Blessed Repose cemetery. One night it arrived outside of this very house, making the final weary mile to its last and ultimate resting place. The winds howled and the thunder boomed. Lightning flashed and the rain poured down. From this very room the sounds of a dreadful music reverberated and keened into the pitch-black, water-drowned night. '*No*,' screamed the thunder and the wind. '*No*,' shrieked the lightning and the rain. The music moaned and howled. Josiah's old moldering bones shook in their coffin. The box rattled in its cart and from out of this very room a flash of lightning burst toward the last mortal remains of Captain Josiah P. Brademas and scorched it to a pile of cinders where it stood." The room was suddenly too quiet. Ophelia held her breath. "So we always say it's a good idea to stay on the right side of old Sir Henry. If you catch my meaning."

"I do indeed," whispered Ophelia. "What do you suggest?"

"Well, so far, I think you've been just

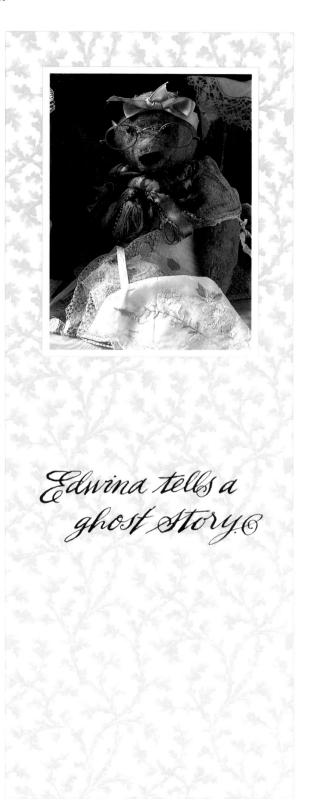

Edwina tells a ghost story.

lovely. These knickknacks here are too beautiful for words. But I was wondering, now, who's going to buy them all?" Edwina asked. "Sir Henry wouldn't like his cloth cut up for naught."

"Why, our customers," explained Ophelia, indignantly.

"What customers?" asked Edwina.

"The ones who'll come to purchase our handiwork," answered Ophelia.

"And who are those going to be?" Edwina continued. "Nobody around here needs anything like this."

"The tourists then," said Zenobia, who had come to inventory Ophelia's creations.

"It's going to take more than a few tourists to buy all this," explained Edwina.

"Once they hear how wonderful our stock is, tourists will come from hundreds of miles away," said Ophelia.

"Who's going to tell them?" asked Edwina.

"I suppose we could advertise," said Ophelia thoughtfully.

"Advertisements are very expensive," said Edwina. "And they don't always succeed."

"We should be able to get some free publicity," Ophelia speculated. "Maybe we could call up the *Times* to cover the rebirth of Bruinyes House."

"And Ernie's butterfly hound," said Zenobia. "And the ghost."

"Why don't we invite the Queen to visit. That would be newsworthy," Ophelia added.

"The Queen is a hard person to get up to the country," observed Edwina.

"But there are lots of other people who would be happy to come for a holiday and see our wonderful things," said Ophelia. "Albert has lots of important friends, and Ernie and Aunt Vita do too. I could invite everyone I know from France and Italy and Japan."

"We could have an enormous party," exclaimed Zenobia. "With food and exhibitions and games. We could have performers and a raffle. It would make all the newspapers, even television."

"What a brilliant idea!" cheered Ophelia. "Zenobia, you're a treasure." Zenobia beamed.

Downstairs, Ricky Jaune, armed with a mop and bucket of water, was halfheartedly making his way across the living room floor.

"Someone will have to get a ladder and go up and do the chandeliers," said Dr. Churchill, eyeing the ceiling. "Why don't you get the ladder," he said to Ricky. "It's in the closet behind the kitchen."

"This is slavery," moaned Ricky.

"It's England, young man," said Dr. Churchill. "Slavery has been abolished for hundreds of years. You are clearly distressed by work. Frankly, I sympathize but I don't really see any way out of it."

Capitulating to the inevitable, Ricky put down the mop and stomped off to the kitchen. "Where's the ladder?" he asked Aunt Vita. She pointed down the hall.

"In the back of the closet behind the library," she advised. "Open the door very carefully. Everything's piled up."

Ricky marched toward the door, grabbed hold of the knob, turned it, and pulled with a disgruntled heave. Pots, pans, irons, old toasters, cricket bats, croquet mallets, vacuum bottles, seltzer siphons, lawn chairs, party tables, and one very large, very unstable ladder flew out all at once. You may wonder how everything fit into the closet in the first place, but it was a very big closet and the English are superb at getting many things into a particularly difficult space. After all, England is not a very large country

Ricky Jaune's mishap

and look what an awful lot of interesting people and things there are there.

Needless to say, Ricky was thrown backward and before you could say, "Oh, what a silly little bear," he was out cold under a mountain of odds and ends, fast asleep, dreaming of Cap d'Antibes (an exquisite beach in the south of France where Ricky had never exactly been but had seen pictures of). Because everyone expected him to make a lot of noise, nobody realized Ricky was knocked out so nobody went to his res-

cue. He was very tired to begin with—the odd goings-on in the old house were beginning to give Ricky nightmares—and since he also had no overriding desire to return to work, he slumbered on hour after hour until the one absolutely inescapable, unalterable fact of a bear's life intruded: hunger. Ricky awoke precisely in time for dinner. He got up, put everything (including the ladder) back, more or less, in the closet and went into the dining room expecting the worst.

"There you are," said Ophelia. "We wondered where you were."

"Lovely work on the chandeliers," said Dr. Churchill. "They really sparkle. But why did you leave all those ribbons and stockings up there?"

Ricky didn't quite know what to say so, trusting his luck, he murmured, "Can I have the stuffing?"

Plans for the party had grown and multiplied. It was now going to be a full-scale carnival with attractions and rides, and booths run by local merchants selling food, antiques, books, and clothing.

"I know a fortune-teller who would come and read your palm," said Edwina.

"Papillon could give butterfly-hunting expeditions," Dr. Churchill proposed.

"I could bake cakes to sell," offered Clarence.

"Anemone could dance," said Albert.

"I could give decorating tips," Conrad volunteered.

"I could give accordion lessons," said a low voice. But no one chose to hear.

"It will be a fabulous party. All the papers, TV, and radio will come. The house will be famous with tourists galore," said Albert.

"I just hope Sir Henry would approve," Ophelia said to herself, with a glance at the dangling ribbons overhead.

The ghost's handiwork?

Ophelia's cure for headaches

VI

I think I have a headache," said Ophelia, her paw on her forehead, sitting up slowly in the big, warm, comforter-strewn four-poster of one of Bruinyes House's many guest bedrooms. The late-morning sun pattered among the pillows and inquired into the counterpane. It had been quite a dinner party.

Perhaps Ophelia had celebrated the night before a bit too exuberantly. But you couldn't rightly blame her. There was much to applaud and Ophelia loved a good time, especially when she herself was responsible for it.

"I think we all ate too much," Clarence concurred. He had a warm, wet towel on his brow which he removed gingerly and handed to Ophelia. "Here, my dear, I got this for you, just testing the temperature."

"The best thing for a headache is wonderful news," said Ophelia.

"What a charming thought. Are you absolutely sure?" asked Clarence.

"No, but it sounds right, doesn't it?" she explained.

"Indeed, perfect. Do you have any?" Clarence was always ready to trust Ophelia's inspiration; it so often proved correct.

"Not immediately, but I'm sure I'll think of something soon."

"I'm positive you will," agreed Clarence, knowing how important it is to support someone at a difficult time.

"I have it!" cried Ophelia. "Let's take the day off. We've been in England three days and it's been nothing but work."

"Tea with the Queen was certainly an honor," Clarence pointed out.

"Yes, of course, but the rest of the time we've run everywhere and worked even harder than at home. I would love to stay in bed for one whole day."

"I'd like to go into town," Clarence mused.

"You know what I mean," said Ophelia. "On a vacation you should do what you want. Let's do it."

"That's the best news I've heard in weeks." Clarence felt his head. "You're a genius, Ophie. My headache's disappeared. Let's tell everyone else."

It was a lucky thing that Ophelia had discovered her cure because everybody was thoroughly sick. Bears just cannot avoid enjoying a party, usually to the point of excess. They are so happy, friendly, and fun to be with, parties just get better and better the more bears you have. Remember that the next time you want to throw a really big wide bright handsome bash: invite plenty of bears. And don't worry that they may stand you up. Bears always come.

Soon everyone was smiling and happy and putting on his or her brightest clothes. Clarence, Zenobia, Albert, Anemone, and Conrad had decided to go to town. Ricky and M. Ritz wanted to explore the neighborhood. Dr. Churchill was anxious to continue his

breakthroughs with Papillon. Ophelia wanted to stay in bed but by the time everyone else began to bustle about and make plans, she was roused into a state of profound inaction. "I think I can just manage to get downstairs and sit by the window if I absolutely try," she confessed.

"I know you, Ophie," said Clarence. "The minute we're all gone, you'll be up and about roaming through Sissinghurst like a native."

"Probably." Ophelia laughed. "But for the moment I don't want to make any plans." Secretly, she hoped to do a little sleuthing on her own. There were too many unexplained occurrences at Bruinyes House for comfort.

Albert borrowed Dr. Churchill's car and drove the others into town. It wasn't a long trip because English towns are very close to each other so if you're not near one town,

invariably you're near another. Zenobia, who was already treating the shop at Bruinyes House with as much care and attention as Bazaar des Bears (and worrying about the cost of the inventory and rate of turnover versus net outflow, overhead, and incidental expenses), was ready for a chance to see some new faces and buy a few postcards. "I haven't written to anyone," she explained. "They live for my letters."

Clarence wanted to scout out the local restaurants. Conrad headed for the antiques shops to look for anything that might be useful in his next production of *Don Carlo*—flags, halberds, habits, perhaps an ancient portcullis. Albert and Anemone tagged along looking for an amusing samovar, hunting horn, trivet, or snuffbox to add to their collection.

Ricky was walking along the lawn and paths of Bruinyes House pretending to be a country squire with all these rolling hills and well-tended grounds his own: the Jaune estates. Lord Jaune, he thought, Viscount Jaune, Earl Jaune, Baron Jaune—it had a ring to it.

It was a cool, sunny morning with enough clouds to conjure a breeze just as soon as you got hot. Ricky wore his sunglasses to be safe and his second-best bow tie, a red silk, to keep up appearances. You didn't really have to dress in the country but it was considered good form. And you never knew whom you might meet.

The gardener, Randolph Fielding, was pruning the roses, clipping off the dead leaves and faded flowers. "Good day to you, Master Ricky," said the gardener, who of course knew everybody's names because Dr. Churchill had told him beforehand. That's part of being a good gardener. "A lovely day, isn't it?"

Randolph Fielding, the gardener

"Yes, absolutely wonderful," said Ricky. "What's the best way to go?"

"That depends on where you want to get to," said Mr. Fielding. "That way," he said, pointing toward a mass of floating green hedgerows, "is the garden. And that way," pointing toward a group of weathered redwood buildings, "is the stables. And that way," pointing over the hills, "is Sissinghurst. I wouldn't recommend the garden, though."

"Why not?" Ricky asked.

"Shrubbery needs pruning," Mr. Fielding said evasively.

"Where do you think I should go?" asked Ricky with becoming modesty and trust.

"Why don't you visit my daughter Penelope. She's just back from school in London. She's working in the stables. Go down and say hullo."

Ricky followed the direction Mr. Fielding's paw indicated to a low, barnlike building at the end of the lawn. He walked to the open door and looked in. A thin figure was trying to lift a large leather saddle. "Can I help you?" asked Ricky.

"Oh please, these are so heavy," she said. Ricky got on one side and Penelope on

Penelope and her dad.

the other and together they heaved the saddle on the back of one of the horses and tightened the girth.

"Would you like to go for a ride?" Penelope asked, smiling.

"Heavens no!" replied Ricky. He looked at her very carefully. Something was strangely familiar but he couldn't decide what. She was dressed in a camisole top, old, baggy maroon knit pants tucked into tall, brown scuffed boots. Her fuzzy brown fur was tied neatly with a ribbon.

"Haven't I seen you before? Have you ever been to Paris?" asked Ricky.

"Not yet, but I'd love to go. Is that an invitation?" Penelope inquired.

"Not exactly." Ricky looked at his paws. She was very pretty. "I just thought I might have seen you on the boulevard Raspail. Or maybe Le Drug Store."

"I was on the train the other night. You fled from me in terror. Was it my perfume?" Penelope laughed.

"I don't believe it. That monster was *you?*" said Ricky, utterly amazed. "It's impossible."

"That was me," she smiled. "Which do you prefer?" Ricky was so confused he simply picked up a piece of straw and tied it into a knot. "That's my London look," Penelope explained. "Down here we're much more casual. I can tell you're a simple boy at heart. But I'm glad you've seen the other me."

Ricky looked up. "Me too," he said. "Would you like to take a walk?"

"Wonderful. They're having a jumble sale down the road. I was going to ride but a walk would be even better. We'll have to take the saddle off the horse, though," laughed Penelope. She loved to laugh.

They took the saddle off and hung it back on its post. They tethered the horse and

locked the stable, then headed down the road.

"Are you sure you're not French?" asked Ricky.

"I doubt it." She smiled. "Are you sure you're not British?"

"I sometimes think I must be somebody else the way everyone yells at me. Maybe I was stolen by pirates or kidnapped by gypsies. I could be British. Or Polynesian."

"I always thought I was Polynesian too. Maybe we were kidnapped by the same pirates?"

They walked along the road and came to a broad lawn filled with tables piled to overflowing with used records, old books, kitchenware, and knickknacks. It was a jumble sale. Ricky and Penelope browsed, picking up bottles and plates and pictures, examining them carefully and then putting them back.

"Here now, young lady and gentleman, this is what you need," said a cheery, red-faced bear in a bright yellow shirt, green suspenders, and blue pants. He held up a

*Penelope and
Ricky Jaune
down at the Stables*

huge slinky accordion that slithered and twisted in his hands. "Only two pounds ten, good as new, better, been played for thirty years, you know it works."

"I've always wanted an accordion," cried Ricky. "My favorite song is 'The Roses of Picardy.'"

"That's my favorite too," cried Penelope.

"There now, it's decided," said the vendor. "Tell you what. I'll throw in this whole beautiful pile of music. What do you say?"

"I really shouldn't," said Ricky, hesitating. "Everyone will laugh at me."

"I won't laugh," Penelope promised.

"I'll take it," said Ricky. "But wrap it up tight so nobody knows."

Ophelia had sat still for exactly three and a half minutes after the others had left, then she jumped out of her chair. She planned to investigate the attics for the source of the strange accordion music but before she could act, Dr. Churchill stopped by.

"Come with us," said Ernie. "Monsieur Ritz and I are going out to train Papillon on another butterfly."

"I think I can smell butterflies too," said M. Ritz. "The yellow ones smell like Limburger. The green ones smell like Belpaese and the white ones smell like Muenster."

"I need some fresh air," agreed Ophelia. "Lead on."

They returned to the field where Papillon had scored his first triumph. As before, it was a sea of butterflies. M. Ritz and the dog smelled butterflies galore and Dr. Churchill called out their names to identify them for future reference. For a while Ophelia watched happily, but soon she found herself wandering away. The planted paths and tree-lined alleys beckoned. Here was a lovely weathered marble statue of a nymph, there was a trellised arbor of flowering wis-

teria or tangled roses mixed red and pink and white. The walks were designed to be circuitous so that no matter where one strayed, some clever vista of grove or planted plot or fountain appeared every few minutes. The British were in love with their gardens and often devoted even more imagination and care to the grounds of their estates than to the houses themselves.

After an hour or so of cheerful, lazy circumambulation, Ophelia thought she should perhaps find her way back to her friends. It seemed logical to believe that any path would ultimately return one to Bruinyes House. So Ophelia was not overly concerned when the farther she walked, the less open and friendly the landscape seemed to be. Rows of hedges and lines of trees confronted her at every turn, hemming her in and directing her steps in an increasingly narrow, twisting route. Through the walls of green she saw she was headed toward a specific goal, a white marble building in a circle of fluffy white-blossomed trees. It was a perfect reproduction of a Greek temple, but in miniature as though built for a child. This was a folly, Ophelia knew, an ornate structure designed solely as an attractive addition to a garden.

It took a while for Ophelia to realize she was lost, that no matter which way she went she never seemed to get anywhere. For she had wandered, quite accidentally, into the maze of Bruinyes House. And she was lost! Ophelia was scared but she didn't panic. She sat down and thought very carefully. I got in, she realized, therefore there must be a way out. She looked all around, up and down. At her feet was one of the beautiful ribbons from the attic. Not too far away was another. There was a trail of ribbons leading off in one direction. She remembered the words "the Ribbon King" written on the

Putting Papillon to the test

Lost in the maze

attic mirror. Clearly, if I follow the ribbons I can't be any worse than I already am, she reasoned, but it does seem funny to have ribbons all the way out here.

"It's not funny at all," said a quiet voice.

"Excuse me," said Ophelia.

"After all, you're the one who's lost. I'm not lost. I know where I am. I look where I'm going," said the voice. "And when somebody helps me out, I don't take it for granted."

"I'm not," said Ophelia in amazement. "I'm truly grateful. Thank you so much, whoever you are."

If Ophelia looked very carefully at the direction of the voice she could just barely make out the shadow of a tall, lean form with a thin aristocratic face and narrow paws and feet, dressed in an immaculately pressed morning coat, bowing. "I am truly honored," said Ophelia, curtsying in return. "Do I have you to thank for the ribbons in the attic, the music on the lawn, and my present rescue?"

"Indeed you have," replied the ghost.

"Dr. Churchill thought it was squirrels, but I was afraid it was Sir Henry."

"Certainly not squirrels." The ghost coughed. "If you will follow the ribbons you will return to your friends. Please be more careful. It has been a pleasure."

"But wait! I want you to come meet the others. And who *are* you?" Ophelia cried at the filmy apparition. With a small, sad smile he bowed once again, and dissolved before Ophelia's very gaze.

Puzzled but relieved, Ophelia went down the particolored path, and soon enough the trees and bushes broadened out and the walls of green gave way to vistas of hills and houses. "I'm saved. I met the ghost!" she cried out and ran toward Ernie and M. Ritz shouting for joy.

"We were just going to look for you," replied Dr. Churchill. "It's very easy to get lost out here. The hills and valleys all look the same."

"I was lost in the maze," Ophelia confessed. "Fortunately the ghost spread a trail of ribbons pointing the way out."

"Nonsense, my dear," chided Dr. Churchill. "Surely you're too old to believe in ghosts."

"Not when they save my life," said Ophelia, ruefully.

"Was it Sir Henry? Weren't you frightened?" Clarence asked, shivering.

"I don't think it was Sir Henry. He seemed far too well behaved for a highwayman, not the least bit menacing."

"Well, whoever it was, I'm just glad you're safe," said Clarence. "In fact, I think we should celebrate. But let's not tell the others about your encounter just yet. It would only make them uneasy, and I don't want anything to spoil our fete tomorrow."

Reluctantly, Ophelia agreed not to mention meeting the ghost until after the party, and M. Ritz and Dr. Churchill were sworn to secrecy as well.

"And now to celebrate your safe return," Clarence said.

"Brie for everyone!" cried M. Ritz.

"But we just celebrated last night," said Ophelia.

"All the more reason not to neglect this extraordinary opportunity to celebrate again so soon," explained Dr. Churchill.

"Yes, that does make sense," agreed M. Ritz, "I think."

"Well then, a small party," said Ophelia. "Just the four of us. And whoever else happens by." She looked over her shoulder toward the hedgerows.

By the time they were on their second wheel of Brie, everybody was there.

Ricky's foolish purchase

VII

THE PREPARATIONS

I can't believe you bought an accordion," said Albert in amazement.

"You can't even whistle," said Conrad. "You have a tin ear."

"Tin, he'd be lucky with tin. I'd say steel or waxed paper or carborundum," snuffled Aunt Vita. "The boy has absolutely no musical talent whatsoever!"

"I'm sure they took you for everything you've got," said Ophelia, laughing. "Did you have to mortgage the shop?"

"I can so whistle. I do not have a tin ear. I only paid two pounds for it and got all this beautiful music thrown in. I'm going to play so wonderfully they'll want me at the Paris Opéra. I'll play with the Rolling Stones," Ricky exclaimed. "What's carborundum?"

Of course it was clear from the moment Ricky returned that he had purchased something especially foolish. Albert finally shamed the boy into unwrapping his treasure for all to see. Anemone asked for a song and regretted it from the first note. Ricky was by no means a natural.

"One accordion player in this house is enough," said Aunt Vita.

"That's right. Ricky can take lessons," suggested Clarence. "Who exactly does play the accordion here?"

"We never found that out," observed Zenobia.

"It's the ghost," said Ophelia.

"There is no ghost," said Aunt Vita and Dr. Churchill. Zenobia gave Ophelia a worried glance. "There *is* a ghost, and he's very kind and friendly," Ophelia insisted, but no one seemed to believe her, except Clarence, who shook his head in warning.

"Did you buy anything, Zenobia?" asked Dr. Churchill, to change the subject.

"I wrote seventeen letters. I left nobody out," said Zenobia with pride. "I even wrote to that nice librarian at the British Museum."

"Did you write to me?" asked Ricky.

"Of course not. You're right here."

"No one ever sends me any letters," said Ricky.

"You never go anywhere," replied Zenobia.

"What do you mean," exclaimed Ricky. "I go everywhere. I went to Japan. I'm in England right now."

"I went to Japan with you," she explained, trying hard to be patient. "We are in England together."

"So where are my letters?" continued Ricky.

"I can't write you any letters unless you are someplace other than where I am." Zenobia sighed.

"Why?" moaned Ricky. "You just don't want to write me any letters. I never get any letters. You write letters to everybody and you don't write me anything, ever."

Zenobia gave up. "I'll write you a letter, the first chance I get."

"A long one," said Ricky enthusiastically,

The correspondents

"filled with lots of juicy gossip and news."

"I promise, I promise," said Zenobia.

"And put a colorful stamp on it, a big one with red and yellow and green. Maybe two or three stamps," Ricky added. Zenobia nodded her head. The things she did for that boy!

The doorbell rang. Ophelia went off to answer it. Early as usual, there were Popie and Marcello, Ophelia's dearest Italian friends. Marcello was the Italian ambassador to France; Popie was an extremely creative international financier, somewhat down on his luck.

"I didn't want to miss it," yelled Marcello as he stepped through the door. "I didn't miss it? Tell me I didn't miss it," and he hugged Ophelia tight enough to cause damage (but didn't).

"You didn't ishy ugh," said Ophelia.

Marcello and Popie with Ophelia

*The new guests
meet Papillon*

"I'm so happy," cheered Marcello.

"I'm happy too," added Popie. "I'm happier." They were both very sturdy from many plates of pasta, and when they were happy the earth shook.

"I'm happiest," yelled Marcello. "Who's here? What can I do? I'll do anything. Just tell me what to do. When do we eat?"

"Dinner's in half an hour. There's lots to do. The party isn't 'til tomorrow," Ophelia explained. "We're having a preparty party."

"Wonderful. Marvelous. Superb," said Popie. "We're the first to arrive. I hate to be late."

"We brought everybody presents. I've missed you so much. I can't believe this house. Wherever did you get it? Is there running water?" Marcello paused for a breath and went on. "I brought you a little something from Rome, just a trifle, a knick-knack. Try it on when everyone else is asleep," he said, handing her a red and green box. "I couldn't come empty-handed. I love parties. How clever of you to have it here, in the middle of nowhere. It's like a treasure hunt: find the party. I got lost sixty times. Do you know how many Bruinyes Houses there are in Sissinghurst? The place is crawling with them. Where do I stay? I must have running water. I brought my own sheets. You look spectacular. It must be the dress. Or is it the hat? What have you done? So *raffiné*. What's for dinner?"

Ophelia managed to cut him off, barely, by pushing him headfirst into the living room to meet everyone else. You couldn't help but love Popie and Marcello, they were so loud and exuberant and generous. They had indeed brought the most wonderful presents for all the bears, including a box full of butterflies for Dr. Churchill which he gleefully ran into his study to classify at once.

"Marcello has thought of the best idea for our festival," said Ophelia after the presents were opened.

"I have, really? I don't remember. How clever I am. What is it?" said Marcello.

"A treasure hunt," replied Ophelia. "We'll hide a big cloth *B* in one of the bushes or a fountain. Whoever finds it will win one of our quilts."

"That will be fun to watch," said Clarence. "Grown men climbing trees."

"You need major events to get the crowds going," said Marcello. "How about chariot races or a beauty contest. Miss Sissinghurst?"

"I hardly think that would be appropriate," sniffed Aunt Vita. "Though I can think of several who might enjoy it."

The bears had a quick dinner—pasta and fresh asparagus (the menu suffered an abrupt change to Italian from English with the arrival of the new guests)—and then work began in earnest on the next day's fete. Tables were carried out and arranged in rows on the lawn. All the wares that had been produced were placed neatly on a large counter, with price tags on every item. Albert and Conrad drew signs in bright, fluorescent colors saying: THE HANDKERCHIEFS ARE A STEAL AT 6 SHILLINGS 10. YOU CAN'T GO WRONG WITH THE PILLOWCASES, TWO FOR 3 POUNDS 7. HAVE YOU THOUGHT ABOUT A NEW BEDSPREAD? GET ONE TODAY, ONLY 50 POUNDS, DUSTCOVERS 4 POUNDS 9.

Anemone and Conrad put together a miniature stage for the performers and musicians. Mr. Fielding brought up several huge pots of flowering plants and masses of cut flowers to be placed at strategic spots inside the house and out. Clarence baked chocolate cakes until there was no more room to put them. Aunt Vita tied ribbons on shortbread cookies and cut the crusts off Ophelia's own special-recipe finger sandwiches.

Les spécialités de la maison

M. Ritz wrapped streamers on all the chandeliers and plumped the cushions by jumping up and down on them. Finally it was all done and everyone sat down exhausted but happy.

"What if it rains?" said Dr. Churchill.

"Oh heavens, no! It can't rain. It mustn't rain," cried Ophelia.

"But it might," said Clarence. "We should be prepared."

"It won't rain," someone said.

"There you go," exclaimed Ophelia. "It won't rain."

"Who said that?" asked Conrad.

"I didn't," answered Ricky, Aunt Vita, Albert, Anemone, Dr. Churchill, Clarence, and M. Ritz.

"Somebody said it," demanded Zenobia.

"Ricky, are you playing games?"

"I'm too tired for games," sighed Ricky. "Honest."

"We can't trust our whole enterprise to a mysterious voice," Dr. Churchill protested.

"I don't see why not," said Ophelia. "It's the ghost. He's perfectly trustworthy."

"If there is a ghost, why can't the rest of us see him?" demanded Zenobia.

"Maybe he's shy," Ophelia said.

"But who is it?" Aunt Vita asked, looking very worried. "Is it Sir Henry?"

"I hope I'm not sleeping in his bedroom," said Ricky, moving closer to Zenobia's comforting side.

"That I can't say," Ophelia announced. "But if he says it won't rain, then it won't."

"Let's go to bed," said Zenobia.

"What a wonderful idea," said Clarence. "I vote yes."

They all did and soon the house was as quiet and dark as the inside of a bread box. But if you looked closely you could see, in the murky gray light shed by the moon into Bruinyes House, a white transparent figure going silently among the tables and stands, the decorations and merchandise, straightening, neatening up the corners, rearranging the piles, and making everything shipshape and perfect for the big day.

Anemone and Conrad plan the gala

Anticipation!

VIII

The day of the fete began with a truly magnificent morning such as English poets write about once every three hundred years. It hadn't rained at all (unprecedented). There wasn't a cloud in the sky (unheard-of). It was warm and dry and sunny (inconceivable). It was an absolutely, utterly perfect day for an outdoor fair.

"You see," said Ophelia, looking out of the window. "I told you it wouldn't rain."

Clarence laughed and threw his pillow into the air. "Ophelia, you're amazing."

Ophelia smiled.

Everything had been done the night before, so all the bears had to do was watch the concessions being set up outside and wait for the crowds. Zenobia, of course, was nervous and pacing the parlor.

"What if nobody comes?" she worried. "What if the train gets lost or the airports are closed? What if it snows? What if Ophelia's ghost scares everyone off?"

"It's not going to snow in the middle of the summer. The trains have run for hundreds of years. If the airports are closed, which they won't be, most of the people are coming from down the road by car. And I still don't believe in ghosts," Conrad explained to no avail. Zenobia sat by the window until the first visitors began to arrive, then she still wasn't happy until they began to buy. Finally, when Ophelia ran out of comforters and sachets and Freddy and Penelope were down to their last shortcakes and scones, and Zenobia sold every last pillowcase and scarf and there hadn't been the slightest hint of accordion music, she was heard to admit in a low mutter, "I think

maybe, just possibly, we might be all right."

A number of people, sadly, did not come. The Queen sent her regrets and a lovely box of divinity fudge that she made herself. Mona Lisa and Schnuffy were too far away (Japan) to fly in for the party, though they sent an exquisite card hand-painted by Schnuffy with a haiku poem composed by Mona: "Parties with new friends / Always bring old friends great joy / Even far away / Love, Schnuffy and Mona." The entire company of the Vienna State Opera sent an autographed picture to Conrad. Heidi and Clafouti sent a huge tin of pâté from Fauchon.

But almost everyone else came. The entire population of Sissinghurst, a large part of Shropshire, and a big wedge of Worcestershire filled the house and grounds to bursting. Booksellers had whole libraries spread out on their tables. Antiques enough to stock a museum spilled over wide swathes of the lawn and patio. Pub owners and food vendors from three counties had come down to purvey their gustatory

delights. Puppeteers performed Punch and Judy, jugglers juggled, musicians played "Greensleeves," "Scarborough Fair," and "Barbara Allen" until the songs ran through your head with nobody playing them. Ricky brought out his accordion and got as far as the second verse of "The Roses of Picardy" before jeers and groans forced him to retreat. Fortunately, at that point Penelope (who had snuck away from Ophelia's booth)

Zenobia's delicious wares

rode up and offered to sell rides on her horse to the children. She insisted that Ricky help her, and he was only too happy to oblige.

Anemone danced the dying swan solo from *Swan Lake*. Marcello drew an exact copy of God giving life to Adam from the Sistine Chapel ceiling in chalk on one of the patio steps, and Popie made a clay replica of the bronze horses from San Marco. Most exciting to the bears was a genuine gypsy, Serena, who told fortunes from Tarot cards or your paw (both for a bargain rate). Ophelia was particularly pleased to hear she would soon be taking a long trip.

"But you're *on* a long trip," exclaimed Zenobia.

"It's always good to plan ahead," said Ophelia.

"Maybe she means you're going home from the trip you're on," suggested Conrad.

"Then she would have said you're going home from a long trip," explained Ophelia. "And she didn't."

"Dear Ophie," laughed Clarence. "You're really only happy in motion."

"I don't believe a bear was meant to stay in one place too long," she observed.

"But what about Bazaar des Bears," said Zenobia, suddenly fearful.

"Bazaar des Bears is not a place. Bazaar des Bears is home. Every bear needs a home," said Ophelia.

"Thank heavens!" said Zenobia, Conrad, Clarence, M. Ritz, and Ricky Jaune.

"That doesn't mean she can't occasionally stray." Ophelia smiled.

It was a glorious carnival filled with excitement, surprises, things to do, see, and eat. Aunt Vita and Dr. Churchill were positively jubilant to see the tremendous success of their venture. They leapt from booth to booth, patted old friends on the back,

thanked merchants and townspeople for their generosity and help, urged visitors to purchase this or that artifact, blanket, sausage, fried fish stick, because—after all—the money was going to a good cause. Indeed, it was very clear now that Bruinyes House was saved. The relief was palpable, not just in Aunt Vita and Dr. Churchill but also among the cameramen and crew of BBC 1, the newspeople from all over England who cheerfully overemphasized the point: this was a sacred part of England. To let it sink into decay and oblivion would be to let a part of the English soul vanish from the world.

"Aren't they going to say something about us?" asked Zenobia.

"They're getting around to it," explained Ricky. "First they have to warm up."

"They've been warming up for half an hour," said Zenobia.

"That's nothing for television," said Ricky. "They can go on for hours without getting to the point."

"Well, I don't have hours," muttered an exasperated Zenobia. "I have work to do. I can't stand around waiting to be interviewed."

"I don't think they want to interview us," whispered Ricky.

"Of course they do. We did everything. We fixed the house. We designed the merchandise. We created the party to launch the store. Of course they want to interview us," exclaimed Zenobia. "Who else would they want to interview?"

"The celebrities," said Ricky Jaune.

"Don't they know we *are* the celebrities," snapped Zenobia.

"Not to television."

"All right, then, who are the celebrities?" Zenobia fairly seethed.

"Albert because he's royalty. The mayor

Bazaar des BearsEast!

Anemone on stage

of the town. Anyone from the movies or theater," explained Ricky.

"But what have they got to do with saving Bruinyes House?"

"Not a lot. But that's television."

"Well, I want nothing to do with it." And Zenobia stomped off to find something to sell.

Two hours later, Ricky Jaune got fifteen seconds on international television, just long enough to smile and tell the world that he was learning to play the accordion. Ophelia got on for twenty-five seconds and told everyone to shop at Bruinyes House if they couldn't come to Bazaar des Bears. Conrad, Clarence, Zenobia, and M. Ritz never got on at all. But somehow they survived.

The treasure hunt began in the early afternoon and lasted almost three hours. In the end the *B* was found by a ninety-five-year-old retired farmer by the name of Herbert Nottingham (yes, distantly related to the sheriff who made so much trouble for Robin Hood). While everyone else climbed trees and poked into bushes and behind armoires, Herbert scraped with his boot at a large pile of broken paving stones. Needless to say the treasure wasn't there, but when Herbert finally finished and realized he had been wrong, he threw his hat so hard against one of the scaffolds holding up a booth that the whole thing came down. The *B* had been hidden on top of one of the poles. It fell right into his hands and for the first time in twenty-nine years he smiled. But just as Dr. Churchill was about to present the prize there was a great commotion.

"Come quickly," cried Edwina, bursting in. "Someone has just gone out of turn at croquet!"

"Is that a crime?" inquired Clarence.

"Take away their ball," suggested Conrad. "Or better yet, their mallet."

"Rap their knuckles," added Aunt Vita.

"That's just it," exclaimed Edwina, pointing excitedly. "They don't have any."

"Mallets?" asked Conrad.

"Knuckles," said Edwina, "or hands, arms, legs, head."

"Then how can they play croquet?" said Ophelia.

"Nobody knows, but however they do it, they're winning," explained Edwina. "Though not necessarily by the rules."

"It must be the ghost," said Ophelia, vindicated at last.

The bears hurried off to see. Sure enough, in the middle of a somewhat desolate croquet court a ball was being hit by a mallet with no discernible source of propulsion.

"I don't know how it can do that," said Dr. Churchill, "and expect to win."

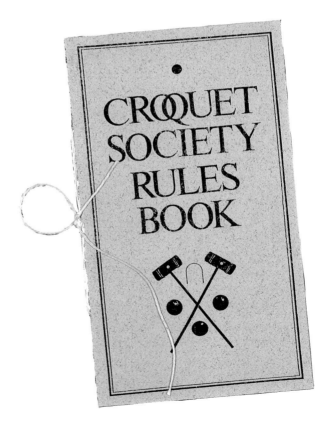

"That's not the point," Zenobia explained. "Something very unnatural is going on. It *must* be the ghost after all."

"Nonsense, there's no such thing as ghosts," said Aunt Vita. "It's one of Ricky's little tricks with magnetism or mirrors. He's been doing them ever since he got here."

"I think it's a ghost. The Croquet Society thinks it's a ghost," Edwina reiterated. "They've marched off in protest. Unfair advantage and all that."

"I know it's the ghost," said Ophelia.

"And I know it's a ghost," said a strange, ominous voice behind them. Everybody turned and looked at a brightly dressed young woman wearing a gaudy turban and holding a crystal ball.

"Who are you?" asked Dr. Churchill.

"Serena, the fortune-teller. Ghosts are my dark business," she answered.

"She's also a wonderful palm reader,"

Ophelia observed.

"Ghosts are more lucrative. Everyone will pay to see a really hideous ghost," explained Serena. "Alas, they are, for the most part, invisible."

"Like this one," said M. Ritz. "Only Ophelia can see him."

"Have you seen strange lights at night, objects flying through the air, heard strange music?" asked Serena.

"We wondered about that," exclaimed Conrad.

"That was the ghost. If it is a good ghost it will help you. If it is unhappy it can cause great uproar and dismay."

"It is a good ghost. He told me so himself. And everything's gone right since we arrived," said Ophelia. "I wish everyone could see him too, so they'd stop being so anxious. It must hurt his feelings being ignored like this."

"I can try to communicate with it if you choose," the fortune-teller offered. "Most ghosts wish to unburden their souls or at least express some dreadful truth. Have there been any messages seen in mirrors or written in blood?"

"A few here and there. We thought it was Ricky," said Clarence.

"Did some horrible fate come to pass, an earthquake, flood, fire?" Serena flung her hands over her eyes.

"Of course not," said Ophelia. "The ghost is being helpful. He's a gentleman."

"You cannot be sure," Serena warned.

"We must meet at midnight in the topmost room. I shall see you then," and in a swirl of skirts and clinking jewelry, she was gone.

"This doesn't look good," said M. Ritz. "I smell trouble."

"I smell expense," said Aunt Vita.

"Did you see that dress," added Zenobia.

"I guess we'd better do what she says," Ophelia capitulated. "I just hope the ghost doesn't mind."

"I could have sworn it was squirrels," confessed Dr. Churchill.

"It probably was squirrels," agreed Clarence, "and also a ghost."

Serena, the gypsy

The Ghost comes forward

IX

It was midnight in the attic of Bruinyes House. A cold wind blew up the stairs and down the halls, rattled the windows, rocked the banisters, and whipped the curtains back and forth. It pushed the rain into the gutters and blew it out the spouts. It hurled the lightning from the heavens, and threw the thunder back.

The bears sat together in the uppermost turret of Bruinyes House and shivered. They were cold and they were damp, but most of all they were scared. It was their very fear that made them jocular. If they did not laugh they would dive under their beds and pray for the dawn. It wasn't so much the presence of a ghost that terrified them. It wasn't the strange gypsy woman and her curious ways. It wasn't the candlelit narrow room, the raging storm, and the cold, clammy air of midnight. It wasn't even the keening wail that the gypsy unleashed every time that silence threatened to descend on the ominous scene. It was purely and simply fear itself which had chosen to fill every corner and crevice of Bruinyes House.

The sewing machines and cutting tables had been pushed aside. The cloth and ribbons were piled up in the corners and against the wall. In the center of the room, around a large circular table, everyone sat holding paws. Serena was looking in her crystal ball and ululating (a very loud form of trilling produced by many African tribes and assorted mystics, guaranteed to scare the wits out of you).

"Does she really have to do that?" asked Aunt Vita.

"I suppose so," said Dr. Churchill. "Otherwise she wouldn't be doing it."

"Not necessarily," said Ophelia.

"Will this take long? I've been trying to classify Marcello's butterflies. There are some remarkable specimens," said Dr. Churchill.

"Let us all join hands," said the gypsy, "and concentrate on the spirit world. Does anyone have a question to ask the dearly departed?"

"I lost a lovely pair of beaded gloves last winter," said Aunt Vita. "Do you possibly know where they may have got?"

"That is not the right kind of question," moaned the gypsy. "You must ask something more ominous and terrifying. Have there been any murders? Who cannot sleep because of dreams in the night filled with blood?"

"I have a terrible time falling asleep," confessed Conrad. "Of course, it might be the liverwurst."

"They are with us," Serena exclaimed. "Speak. Tell us. We will listen!" There was a moment of silence and then:

"I'm so happy you all could come. It's been so lovely having you about."

"You see," cried Ophelia. "I told you it was a good ghost. A gentleman."

At the Séance

"A gentleman's gentleman," said the ghost. "Gervyse Shales, servant to Sir Henry. He is very pleased at what you've done."

"What wonderful news," exclaimed Dr. Churchill. "I've often thought old Sir Henry was disappointed in us."

"He understood your difficulties and sent me to help. He would have come himself but he's on an especially long and dangerous voyage."

"So you're the butler," said Aunt Vita. "How wonderful, a ghost butler, does all the work, needs no food or money. Do you have a brother for my daughter in Shropshire?"

"Why did you write the message in the mirror?" demanded Ricky.

"A small joke," the ghost replied.

"Thank you again for saving me in the maze and for all your help with our store and renovations," said Ophelia.

"It was my pleasure," Gervyse replied. "Thank you for restoring my house. It is dear to me even beyond my life."

"How remarkable," Clarence cheered. "To be so devoted to a house."

"We British value deeply our country and its treasures," said Albert. "It's one of the reasons we have survived and prospered."

"Surely there's something we can do for you," Aunt Vita offered. "Within reason."

"Well, now that you mention it," admitted the ghost. "It would be nice to have a small computer, a Commodore or a Macintosh, an IBM PC would be lovely, just for the video games and perhaps a little late-night hacking. You'd have to run a phone line up to the attic, of course, and throw in a modem, and a printer would be nice."

Dr. Churchill gulped. "Isn't that a bit extravagant?"

"Not really. It's tax deductible, a business expense. Once the store starts cleaning up and the visitors crowd in, you'll need it for the bookkeeping, flowcharts, word-processing. It can do all your mass marketing, direct mail. You won't know how you lived without it."

"He's right, you know," remarked Ophelia. "I'd love one for Bazaar des Bears. It's the future."

"Speak for yourself," snapped Zenobia.

"It would also be nice to have a telly. Just for the educational shows and reruns of *The Avengers*," Gervyse added.

"Of course," said Dr. Churchill. "I'll give you mine. Never watch it anymore since *Wild Kingdom* went off."

"Are you going to be here much longer?" inquired Aunt Vita.

"As long as I'm needed I'll be here. Once repairs are made and the shop is prospering, I'll depart," explained Gervyse. "It's not as if I don't have things to do other than floors."

"We understand," said Albert. "We're all very grateful. Thank you."

"Can you teach me to play the accordion?" asked Ricky.

"I'll try. But it's not going to be easy," said the ghost. "And now, if you don't mind, I'd like to get some sleep. It's past my bedtime."

The bears got up from the table. "I guess that successfully concludes another difficult case," noted Dr. Churchill.

"What do you mean?" asked Conrad.

"Why once again, the butler did it."

Everyone laughed.

For a change Ophelia slept late, and even Zenobia let the late-morning sun creep into her eyes before tidying up her room and going down for breakfast. There was a profound feeling of satisfaction at Bruinyes House this day. The party had raised plenty

A quiet moment alone

of money to begin the major repairs. There was such a demand for Ophelia's creations that the store could barely keep them in stock. Aunt Vita hired Edwina full-time to turn them out as fast as she could. And if people came to the store in the conservatory, they would certainly stay for tea and chocolate cake in the restaurant and perhaps take the full tour. The black days of Bruinyes House were over, thanks to Ophe-lia and her friends. As she was mulling over these cheerful thoughts under her counter-pane, Ophelia heard a wild scream. At first she imagined some terrible event: had Sir Henry returned? But the scream was fol-lowed by Dr. Churchill's voice distinctly uttering hurrahs and "I've found it, a mira-cle, never before seen, unique, spectacu-lar!" and she knew it was some further breakthrough in the doctor's work.

Dr. Churchill's big discovery

"We'd better go downstairs and see what it is, Ophie," said Clarence.

"We could wait 'til he comes up here. I'm sure he's on his way," she replied. And indeed in three seconds the door was flung open and in strode Dr. Churchill, holding aloft a tiny green dot between two fingers.

"I've found it. I've found it. An entirely new butterfly. Isn't it magnificent?" he said.

"Where is it? I can't even see it," laughed Clarence.

"It's a beauty, a butterfly never before discovered. Marcello brought it from Rome. It was at the bottom of the box. I just got to it. I couldn't believe it. You look, Ophie. You're a lady," exclaimed Dr. Churchill.

Ophelia peered at the tiny bit of emerald velvet that seemed to glow at the end of Dr. Churchill's fingers. "It's magnificent. I'm so excited. What do we do?"

"Why, first we have to name it. I hadn't even thought of that. What shall we call it?" asked Dr. Churchill.

"The green Churchill, I would think," said Clarence. "After all, you discovered it. Or should we name it after Marcello?"

"I know what we'll do!" cheered Dr. Churchill. "Of course, it's so simple, like all really great truths. I name this butterfly the Emerald Ophelia after my dearest friend and the savior of Bruinyes House. It's the least I can do for the most wonderful bear in the world."

"I'm speechless," gasped Ophelia, beaming with joy. "I really don't know what to say."

"Let's tell everyone else," shouted Dr. Churchill, and he ran off to do just that.

"How does it feel to be a butterfly?" Clarence asked.

"About the same as it does to be a bear," Ophelia replied. "I still don't have wings."

"Have you looked? Are you absolutely

the Emerald Ophelia

sure?" And Clarence turned her around to check.

Breakfast was very exciting once everyone finally made it downstairs. There was the news of Dr. Churchill's discovery, and of course so many stories to tell about last night's séance and yesterday's festival and all the many wonderful experiences the bears had had in England. Throughout the happy meal Gervyse hovered discreetly over the table, passing the sugar bowl and refilling the cream pitcher.

"I'll miss this beautiful place," said Ophelia.

"You should come back here often," suggested Aunt Vita. "I think of you as one of the owners. If it hadn't been for you, this house would have been gone in a year."

"Why don't you open a Bazaar des Bears in England," said Albert. "The Queen loves your things. You're a big hit in Sissinghurst. Go all the way. Go international."

"I'm up to my eyelashes in work just running the Paris store. How could I run two?" groaned Ophelia.

"We'd love to see more of you," added

Celebrating in the conservatory

Anemone. "Maybe we could open a branch of Hanover House in Paris."

"That would be lovely," cheered Zenobia. "There's always room for quality on the rue du Bac."

"I have it," exclaimed Dr. Churchill. "I'm going to Rome to find out where Marcello found this butterfly. I have to discover where Emerald Ophelia lives, what it eats, what its habits are. Why don't you come with me?"

"We already know what Emerald Ophelia eats," said Clarence. "Foie gras, chocolate cake, and champagne."

"And its habits are far too scandalous to detail in any professional publication," added Conrad.

"And it lives on rue du Bac and owns a store that survives on the blood, sweat, and tears of one Zenobia Onassis, not that anyone ever mentions it," Zenobia threw in.

"Oh, Zenobia, we love you. Don't I say it a million times a day? Where would we be without you?" cried Ophelia.

"I suppose you do. But I just like to hear it again," said Zenobia, smiling.

"Did I hear someone say Rome?" boomed Marcello, finally coming down the stairs with Popie in tow.

"You did indeed," said Dr. Churchill. "I'm going there as soon as I can, and I thought it would be lovely if Ophelia came to see her butterflies in their natural habitat."

"You must. You have to. I insist. It's decided. When do we leave?" Marcello fairly bubbled over.

"I'd love to go," cheered Ophelia, "but we have to get back to the store to make sure everything is all right."

"We'll probably have to put all the handkerchiefs back on the handkerchief shelves and take the pillowcases off the radiators and find the sachets wherever Heidi hid

them," added Zenobia.

"That can't take very long," said Dr. Churchill. "I'll make hotel reservations at the Grand."

"And I'll call up all the best restaurants and make sure we have fabulous tables," Marcello exclaimed.

"Can Penelope come too?" asked Ricky.

"That cute young thing with the horse?" asked Clarence. "That was fast."

"Ricky's growing up," said Ophelia.

"She's always wanted to travel. I invited her to Paris," said Ricky softly.

"Well, I like her," said Conrad. "She's got style. Let her come along."

"I hear Rome is truly lovely in the fall," added Albert.

"Rome is truly lovely always," said Marcello impassionedly.

"Perhaps I can find some matter of state that urgently requires my personal attention in Italy," Albert speculated.

"I'd love to see the new fashions," said Anemone.

"Enough. I'm convinced. Let me catch my breath. We'll go," cried Ophelia. "But first things first."

"And what's that?" asked Clarence, knowing full well what it was.

"Hot chocolate all around," Ophelia said.

Gervyse smiled with satisfaction and drifted into the kitchen to start another pot.

An invitation to Italy

Edwina Takes Stock

X

HOME

Paris is always most beautiful when you've come home.

Bazaar des Bears was the same bustling, tidy store that Ophelia had left even if she felt ten years had gone by. We've done so much, thought Ophelia, but so little really changes. Just as it should be. Isn't that wonderful.

The mail arrived as late as ever on Mondays and there was a letter from Aunt Vita confirming the tremendous success of Bruinyes House's gift shop and restaurant. Carpenters were hard at work restoring the floors and ceilings. Torn curtains were being replaced and worn furniture repaired. In a few weeks the house would be as beautiful and elegant as any mansion in England. No trace of Gervyse had been spotted since Ophelia's departure, much to her relief.

Perhaps the Bazaar could use a bit of redecorating and renovation. Never, thought Ophelia. Bazaar des Bears was perfect the way it was. It just got better and better the more dust and fading that time bequeathed to it.

"Are you looking forward to our trip to Rome, Zenobia?"

"Heavens, Ophie! I don't know how you find the strength. I've just unpacked," said Zenobia.

"It *is* nice to be back, at least for a while," Ophelia agreed. She looked out on the soft, tree-lined streets of Paris, smelled the fresh croissant on the table near the steaming cup of mint tea. Clarence was writing a long article on the culinary particularities of rural England. The sound of his typewriter echoed from the study. Ricky

was laboring against a two-week accumulation of dust in the storeroom. M. Ritz had roused a cat from behind the bath towels. Heidi swore it must have snuck in while she was out for a quick poetry reading.

"Do you think Bazaar des Bears will ever have a ghost?" asked Zenobia.

"It already does," laughed Ophelia. "I haven't overindulged in three days. I'm a shadow." She opened the newspaper and skimmed the morning's headlines. "Oh my stars! I'm in the paper," she shouted. Zenobia came running in. Sure enough, there on the front page was Ophelia's picture in full color and underneath in bold letters, PROMINENT PARIS SHOPKEEPER HAS BUTTERFLY NAMED FOR HER. The whole story was there. Dr. Churchill must have told the press.

"Ophie, you're famous!" cried Zenobia.

Ophelia laughed. "So I am, Zenobia. So I am."

Ophelia B. Wise

Clarence

Aunt Vita

Zenobia Onassis

Ricky Jaune

Conrad

Dr Ernest Churchill

W. Ritz

Papillon

Edwina and Freddy ©

Randolph Fielding

Penelope Fielding

Serena

Anemone and Albert

Marcello

Popie

Acknowledgments

I would like to extend a special thank you to all the people who have been part of *Ophelia's English Adventure:*

Carol Leslie, for her belief and her expertise, who has never stinted in her time or efforts on my behalf; Fred and Catherine Leslie, who have shared Carol's time so generously with me.

Pam Krauss, my editor, whose steadfastness and humor, as well as understanding and insight, have made Ophelia's journey a delight.

Alf Collins, who always has been willing and able to help and who helps Ophelia start off on the right foot.

Shirley Collins, who has always had the time and energy to help me in all of my endeavors, even when she didn't have the time and energy to spare. Both Alf and Shirley are like fairy godparents to Ophie.

Jon Etra, whose good spirits, humor, speed, and willingness to become a part of Ophelia's entourage have provided us all with many smiles.

Marsha Burns, for her time and her understanding of my style and my desire to share this appreciation with others. Without her ability and talent and perception, it would not have been possible to have this translated to film.

Michael Burns, who has kept his humor and his perceptive eye as sharply tuned for this project as for the others. I especially thank him for not allowing all the chaos and disorder in the studio to deter his wit and good nature.

Tim Girvin, who completely understands the concept of Ophelia and who has always managed to find the time in his manic schedule to do something extra on our behalf. His vision and guidance and his staff have become an important part of Ophelia's life.

Tim Girvin Design, Inc., especially Stephen Pannone for his steady, patient attentiveness to all the details of Ophie's style and clutter; Peg Ogle, and all the staff for their indulgence and support; and Rachel Norton for her behind-the-scenes work and good humor.

Randy Hayes, for his "construction" of Bruinyes House and his quiet support of these projects.

Bruce Guenther for finding Bruinyes House in his library and sharing it with us.

Joe McDonnal, whose chocolate cakes taste as good as they look.

Carol Winship of Madame & Co. for the generous gift of Ophelia's court dress.

Susan Ohlson-Elo for letting Fielding and Ricky raid her garden.

Beverly McDevitt for always finding just the right trinkets for Ophelia and her friends.

Richard Tyler Nelson, aka Ricky, for his chintz collection.

Alexis Poliakoff of Pixi & Cie, Paris, for the creation of Conrad's teeny lead bears.

Morri Hart for Ricky's accordion and music lessons.

Karen Bell for the gift of Lady Jane Padelford's dress for Penelope.

Diane Millican, Wayne Wilson, Richard Tyler Nelson, and Nelly Myhre for minding the Bazaar des Bears while this project was being completed, and all the loyal fans and customers who have been patient and good natured about the slightly dotty character of the shop.

Carol Southern and Clarkson N. Potter, Inc., for their belief and guidance in Ophelia's growth. Carol, whose eye and instinct have helped create these lovely books, and Clarkson N. Potter, Inc., whose imprint means a very special style and quality. I am extremely pleased and grateful to be associated with this company.

Gael Towey for her art direction and her openness to Ophelia's peculiar and particular style.

Missy Schueneman, Harvey-Jane Kowal, and True Sims, for invaluable assistance.

There are many others who deserve recognition in a project such as this. There is not space to acknowledge them all, but I would also like to especially thank the sales reps for the Crown Publishing Group, the book-sellers, the buyers and readers of books, for they all contribute to my books and help perpetuate the life of publishing and the distribution of ideas.